MALORIE BLACKMAN

Dead Gorgeous

CORGI BOOKS

BIRMINGHAM LIBRARIES

SHELDON

DEAD GORGEOUS
A CORGI BOOK 0552 54633X

First published in Great Britain by Doubleday,
an imprint of Random House Children's Books

Doubleday edition published 2002
Corgi edition published 2003

1 3 5 7 9 10 8 6 4 2

Copyright © Oneta Malorie Blackman, 2002
Cover photography © Getty; design: www.hen.uk.com

The right of Malorie Blackman to be identified as the author of this work has been
asserted in accordance with the Copyright, Designs and Patents Act 1988.

All rights reserved. No part of this publication may be reproduced, stored
in a retrieval system, or transmitted in any form or by any means, electronic,
mechanical, photocopying, recording or otherwise, without the prior permission
of the publishers.

Papers used by Random House Children's Books are natural, recyclable products
made from wood grown in sustainable forests. The manufacturing processes conform
to the environmental regulations of the country of origin.

Corgi Books are published by Random House Children's Books,
61–63 Uxbridge Road, London W5 5SA,
a division of The Random House Group Ltd,
in Australia by Random House Australia (Pty) Ltd,
20 Alfred Street, Milsons Point, Sydney, NSW 2061, Australia,
in New Zealand by Random House New Zealand Ltd,
18 Poland Road, Glenfield, Auckland 10, New Zealand,
and in South Africa by Random House (Pty) Ltd,
Endulini, 5A Jubilee Road, Parktown 2193, South Africa

THE RANDOM HOUSE GROUP Limited Reg. No. 954009
www.kidsatrandomhouse.co.uk

A CIP catalogue record for this book is available from the British Library.

Printed and bound in Denmark by
Nørhaven Paperback A/S, Viborg

To Neil and Lizzy with love

1. Liam

A storm was coming. I could smell it in the brackish air, hear it in the growl of the waves, see it in the darkening clouds. Josh picked up a stone and tried to skim it across the foaming water. It sank immediately. A wave raced up the beach towards us as if in protest.

Josh laughed and picked up another stone. 'Wow! Look at that!'

A salt tang caught at the back of my throat and I had to cough slightly to clear it before I could speak.

'Look! Look!' Josh pointed.

'At what?'

'The sea.'

'What about it?'

'It's like a huge pot of spaghetti, boiling and bubbling!'

I looked away and shook my head, biting back on the words that just itched to leave my mouth.

'Amazing! Check the sky!' Josh continued.

I automatically looked up at the strange yellowy-grey clouds. It was as if the tops of the clouds were solid and on fire and all the resultant soot and ash were falling to the bottom of them. It was quite common to see the clouds like that over the coast where we lived but I'd never seen them like that anywhere else, and certainly not inland. Not that I'd been to that many places. Not that I'd been anywhere really. The sky matched my mood. Unsettled. Restless.

'What about the sky?' I said, unable to keep the impatience out of my voice.

'Isn't it terrific? Like . . . like . . .'

'Oh, for heaven's sake, Josh. Not again,' I snapped like an old elastic band. 'Why're you always going on about the skylight and

the twilight and the moonlight? No wonder you're always getting picked on at school.'

Josh looked up at me like a wounded dog I'd kicked when he was down. 'I like . . . looking at things.'

'Fine. But that's no reason to drip on like a snotty tissue about them,' I said viciously.

Josh winced at my words and I wasn't sorry. I was glad. I liked to look at things too, but you didn't hear me going on like a girly about them. Josh had to toughen up – fast. I wouldn't always be there to watch his back at school, or anywhere else for that matter. Didn't he understand that?

'I'll shut up then,' Josh replied quietly.

'Thank you,' I said. 'I'd appreciate it.'

Josh's nose began to run. Another reason why my brother always gets picked on. Whenever he's upset, his nose dribbles. It drives me crazy.

'Wipe your nose,' I ordered.

Josh swiped the sleeve of his jumper across his face. He picked up another stone and skimmed it across the water. After a moment I picked up a stone, my hand clenching tightly around its icy smoothness. I knew I was just taking out my bad mood on my brother, but who else was there?

No one.

I shook my head.

My whole life was so pointless. It didn't matter. I didn't matter. I was like one of the small pebbles on the beach, battered smooth by day after month after year of wave upon wave. Except in my case, the wave was my dad. He picked on and criticized and disapproved and condemned every breath I took, until the effect was just the same. I was battered smooth, but that was only on the outside. Inside I was rough and jagged and all corners. And Josh was the only one I could hurt. So I often did. And as much as I hated myself afterwards, it never stopped me from doing it again. And again.

I clenched the stone in my hand even more tightly. Josh sniffed beside me. I wanted to turn to him and hug him and hold him and tell him that he was my brother and that meant something to me. But I didn't. We stood there, together but apart as it began to rain. No gradual build-up from a light spray, but great beads of icy water as big as my fingernails. We were soaked in seconds. The waves lashed up the beach, laughing at us. Or maybe they were angry with us. Or maybe they couldn't care less one way or the other. We picked up smooth stones and skimmed them across the rough water as the storm bashed at us.

It was better than going home.

Sooner or later, we'd have to turn round and head back. If we were lucky, Dad would be round the pub and we'd be able to change our clothes without ructions. If we were lucky. And once again, it'd be left to me to cook up some pasta or some bacon, beans and toast for dinner – which was OK as long as we could eat our dinner in peace before Dad got home. I turned to look at Josh, wondering what he was thinking. As if he sensed me watching him, he wiped his nose again with his sleeve. It was raining quite hard now. The yellow tinge to the clouds had disappeared. Now there was only dark charcoal-grey.

'Come on, Josh,' I shouted above the noise of the waves and the rain. 'Time to head back.'

'Liam, I don't want to go home,' he shouted back.

'Come on.' I started walking up the beach. I didn't need to turn round to know that my brother was standing there watching me. 'Come on, or I'll leave you to it,' I yelled.

Josh started to follow me. I slowed down so that he could catch up. When at last he did, I turned round to him and smiled. He smiled back. Without warning, I grabbed him and put him in a headlock.

'Get off!' he shouted.

After messing up his short locks good and proper, I let him go. Josh had to take a step forward, his hands stretched out before him to stop himself from falling. He sprang up and grinned at me. And just like that, some of the weight was lifted from my shoulders. But not much. And not for long.

'Time to go home,' I sighed.

Josh's smile vanished. And I'd done that. I was always the one to wipe the smile from his face. Sometimes, I really hated being the older brother. Sometimes, I wondered how it would feel to just be me. By myself. No one else to consider. No one else to worry about. Just the thought of it made me ache inside. To be on my own and left alone. Now that would be a real slice of heaven.

2. Nova and Her Dad

Nova had to read the wretched notice her dad had just put on the hotel notice board twice before the full horror of it sank in. What had she done to deserve such a father? Was she someone despicably mean in another life? Just who had she cheesed off? Obviously someone really high up in the pecking order of things, because she was sure paying for it now. It was like every night, Dad dreamed up unique, bizarre and very effective ways to embarrass the hell out of her. And the trouble was, he always succeeded. Nova sighed – one of the deep, long-suffering sighs that she was rightly proud of. She stretched out a hand to remove the notice.

'Nova, don't even think about it,' Dad called out, leaning over the reception desk.

'Dad, you can't leave that there.'

'Why not?'

'Anyone thinking of staying here will think this place is a nut-house, that's why.'

'Any new guests will be impressed by the hygiene standards at our hotel.'

'New guests? Dream on!' Nova muttered. She scowled at Dad's notice. It had to come down. Embarrassing didn't even come close to describing it.

POLITE NOTICE TO ALL GUESTS OF
PHOENIX MANOR

There are some devices which are being underused in this hotel due to an obvious lack of knowledge or

---

technical awareness. I realize that these features come without a user guide, so I thought I might offer some advice.

* The white or wooden handle on the rear wall of each toilet cubicle is not decorative, nor is it the handle of a fruit machine or a firing mechanism for an ejector seat. It has the express function of sending your sausage to the seaside. No matter how proud you may be of the fibre content of your diet, we at this hotel don't want to see the evidence. Flush the ruddy thing!

* Loobrushaphobia continues to be a real problem for some of you. Hold the narrow white or wood-veneer end of the brush and use the bristly end to remove whatever excreta may have avoided 'the flush' (see above).

* When you use the last piece of toilet paper in the dispenser, it would be a noble, charitable and friendly act to replace it from the large stock provided in each bathroom. Please do NOT phone me or any member of my family at Omigod o'clock in the early hours of the morning and ask where the spare toilet rolls are, as happened two nights ago. And if you do run out of toilet paper and find there is no more available in your current location, please do NOT shuffle down to the reception desk with your trousers around your ankles – yes, you, Mr Burntwood. (My wife is still having nightmares.)

* The fact that fresh urine is almost sterile does not entirely mitigate the practice of spraying it around the toilet seat and/or floor like some randy tomcat. In other words, 'If you sprinkle when you tinkle, keep it neat and wipe the seat.'

> If there are any technical issues for which you require further information, please call me on ext. 100 or try www.social.hygiene/how-to-use-the-ruddy-toilet.bum
>
> Tyler Clibbens – Hotel Owner/Manager/General Dogsbody

Nova stretched out a hand towards it.

'Nova, I'm watching you,' Dad yelled, leaning even further over his desk.

'Dad, please.' Nova was desperate. 'Besides, you don't want Mum to see this, do you?'

'So what if she does?' Dad looked around furtively. He stood upright, shoulders squared, lips pursed and set. 'Besides, what I say goes.'

'Only when Mum isn't here,' replied Nova.

'Well, she's not here now so that notice stays. The job's a good 'un! Leave it alone.'

Nova recognized that belligerent tone of voice. She was familiar with the gritty, stern look. She had thought that throwing Mum into the conversation would make Dad back down – it usually did – but he was obviously having one of his 'I'm the man and not under my wife's thumb' moments! Nova couldn't help shaking her head at the notice one last time, before turning to make her way to the kitchen.

Mr Jackman bumped into her and carried on walking without saying a word.

'Excuse me all over the place,' Nova huffed at him.

Mr Jackman hadn't altered his pace one bit. Nova didn't even know if he'd heard her. What was that man's problem? He shuffled around the hotel as if he had the weight of the world on his shoulders. He wasn't even that old. Nova didn't think he'd reached his thirties yet. Early to middle twenties at the most. But he moved like a man at least three times his age. If he tried smiling occasionally he might actually be passable. Short, dark-brown hair, and once, when he'd actually looked at her rather than slinking past, head down, she'd noticed with a start that he had one brown eye and one dark blue. The start was because he'd been at the hotel for a few days by then and it was the first time Nova had caught a clear glimpse of his eyes. She had never seen a mixed race guy with different coloured eyes before. It made Mr Jackman seem even more mysterious.

Now he'd been in the hotel for over a week and when he did put in an appearance – which wasn't often – he always wore immaculate black jeans and a T-shirt, usually white, even in the unusually chilly autumn weather.

'Ah, Mr Jackman, will you be staying on with us for a while longer?' Dad called out, leaning over the reception desk and craning his neck.

Mr Jackman nodded and carried on towards the stairs.

'Can you give me some idea how long you'll be with us?' Dad leaned out even further, one hand waving to attract Mr Jackman's attention.

But the initial nod was all Dad was going to get. Mr Jackman walked up the stairs as if Dad hadn't spoken. As if Dad wasn't even there.

'Er ... Mr Jackman ... Mr — Arrggghhhh!' Dad tipped right over the reception desk to land in a heap on the other side.

'Hello, Nova.'

Nova jumped at the sound of the voice behind her. She whipped round, surprised then not surprised to see Miss Dawn standing behind her. Both Miss Dawn and her companion, Miss Eve, had the weirdest knack of appearing behind you almost out of nowhere. Miss Dawn was an elderly black woman, her black hair streaked with honey-brown and burgundy highlights. She was about as tall as Nova's sister, Rainbow, though Miss Eve was taller.

'He's a strange man, isn't he?' said Miss Dawn.

'Are you talking about my dad or Mr Jackman?'

Miss Dawn smiled in Dad's direction, watching as he cursed up a blue streak while he struggled to his feet. She turned to watch Mr Jackman's back disappear round a bend in the stairs. 'Well, in this instance I was referring to Mr Jackman.'

'He's not very friendly, is he?' Nova said.

'Maybe he's got a lot on his mind,' Miss Dawn suggested.

'And all of it bad, from the look on his face.'

'What he needs is a good friend, my dear. Someone like you,' said Miss Dawn.

'I'm sure the very last thing he wants is to be bothered by me.'

'Don't you believe it. We all need someone to talk to, someone to share things with and sometimes . . .'

'Yeah?'

'Sometimes, no one sees things more clearly than a child.'

'Excuse me, I'm not a child. I'm nearly thirteen.' Nova bristled.

'Oh, of course, my dear. My mistake.' Miss Dawn's eyes twinkled. 'My point is just that sometimes younger ones like you see more clearly than us . . . wrinklies.'

'Tell that to my dad – ' Nova indicated with her head – 'then maybe he'll let me take down that notice.'

'Oh, no! You don't want to take that down. Your father's quite right, my dear.'

'But . . . but it's *embarrassing*!'

'What's embarrassing about using the toilet?' asked Miss Dawn with perfect seriousness. 'It's something to celebrate rather than be ashamed of. We all do it! And toilets are a fantastic invention. So useful. So *comfortable*!'

Nova's face grew hotter by the second. That was not the sort of thing old women should talk about. 'If you say so.' She took a discreet but wary step backwards.

'I do! I've spent many a happy hour sitting on the toilet, reading or sewing or just contemplating the infinite!'

'Er . . . I think I hear Mum calling me. Bye!' Nova turned and raced for the kitchen.

'Nova, don't run!' Dad yelled. 'Health and safety!'

'I wasn't about to give you a graphic demonstration, my dear,' Miss Dawn called out. 'I was just talking about them, that's all.'

Nova didn't stop running until she'd reached the kitchen. If it weren't for the weird guests at the hotel and the even more weird behaviour of her dad, the hotel might actually be a reasonable place to hang out!

3. Nova and Her Mum

'When I was at school, my cookery teacher told us the secret to rolling out good pastry was "Short, sharp strokes away from you! Short, sharp strokes away from you."' Mum matched the words to the actions, her hands on the rolling pin moving in brisk, precise strokes across the pastry on the kitchen table. 'And I find it actually works! I've never rolled out uneven pastry in my life!'

Nova entered the kitchen, only to stop short at the sound of her mum's voice. Mum was a cookery superstar again! Whenever she was alone in the kitchen, she always pretended to be some really famous cook whose every culinary move was watched by millions to copy, learn from and enjoy.

'And I find there's something very soothing about cooking foods high in carbohydrates. Beating cakes. Kneading dough. Rolling pastry. Very therapeutic. Very satisfying,' Mum continued, totally unaware that she was being watched. 'Take this pastry I'm rolling, for instance. Now, the guests brave enough – or broke enough – to eat dinner here may say that my puff pastry is as light as a brick, but they're missing the point. Making pastry stops me from throttling some of them. Beating cake mixture works out all the little stresses and strains of everyday life. And as for kneading bread dough – now that's a life saver. I even keep batches of bread dough in the fridge in case of emergencies. I have a little song I made up which goes to the heart of what I'm trying to say. It goes like this.' Turning her head away from the pastry before her, Mum coughed a couple of times to clear her throat before she began:

> *'When the kids start,*
> *When the bills come,*
> *When the guests complain.*
> *I simply remember where I've put my dough,*
> *And then I'm as right*
> *As rain!*

'Oh, yes, there's nothing like a big dollop of bread dough,' Mum concluded.

'Mum, that's about seventeen signs of madness all rolled into one, that is!'

Mum jumped so high, Nova thought she'd have to scrape her off the ceiling. 'It's not polite to listen to private conversations,' Mum ranted, when her feet touched the ground again.

'And it's not sane to pretend you're being filmed every time you break out a saucepan,' Nova pointed out.

'Was there something in particular you wanted or are you just here to make my life a misery?' Mum asked.

'What're you doing?' Nova came further into the room.

'Making pastry, dear. What does it look like?'

'Who cheesed you off then?'

'No one. Sometimes I make pastry because I'm cooking something that requires pastry.' Mum frowned. 'Besides, you're the one who's got a funny look on your face.'

'No I haven't.'

'Yes you have. Your eyebrows are knotted together so tightly, it'd take Alexander the Great to sort them out.'

'Who's he then? A footballer?' grinned Nova.

Mum shook her head. 'What do they teach you at school these days?'

'Things that are far more useful than the dreary stuff you learned,' Nova replied. 'And I know who Alexander the Great was. He was the son of Alexander the Average.'

'You were telling me why you've got a face on?' Mum said patiently.

'I had to get away from Miss Dawn.'

'Why?'

'She was going on and on about toilets and how lucky we are that they're so comfortable!'

Mum burst out laughing.

'I like her but she is really strange.' Nova shook her head.

'She's in the perfect place then. Strange is what we do best at this hotel,' said Mum.

'Yeah, but there's something very odd about her. And that other woman, Miss Eve. Why do they travel around together? They're always sniping at each other,' Nova wondered out loud.

'At least they don't stab each other in the back,' Mum pointed out. 'They're nasty to each other's faces.'

'But why go around together then?'

'Why not? And at that age, maybe it's better than being alone.'

'Is it?' said Nova.

Mum shrugged. 'Some people will do some really foolish things or put up with a great deal rather than be lonely.'

'Would you?' Nova asked.

Mum considered. 'No, I don't think so.'

'I don't think I would either.'

Mother and daughter exchanged a smile of perfect understanding.

'D'you want a snack?' asked Mum. 'I've bought some

rock buns or there're some doughnuts next to the bread bin.'

'No thanks.'

'Not hungry?'

'Not especially,' Nova replied.

'You never are,' said Mum. 'You only ever eat at meal times – that I've seen, anyway.'

'That's good, isn't it?'

'Yeah, but it's not normal. Not for a twelve-year-old at any rate!'

'I'm the most normal one in this hotel,' Nova said indignantly.

'Which isn't saying much!'

'True,' Nova agreed with a grin.

Mum's smile faded. 'So why d'you never eat snacks?'

Nova sighed with impatience. 'I do eat snacks. I stuff myself with snacks.'

At Mum's raised eyebrows, Nova insisted, 'It's true.'

'You don't seem to have much of a sweet tooth either. It's not natural,' said Mum, more to herself than otherwise.

'Oh, for heaven's sake!' Nova marched over to the bread bin and helped herself to a jam doughnut from the paper bag next to it. She took a huge bite out of it, chewing rapidly as she said, 'See!'

'Yes, dear.' Mum smiled and returned to her pastry. Nova finished her doughnut in four bites before licking her sugary fingers clean like a cat licking its paws.

'Want another one?' asked Mum.

'Maybe later.' Nova drifted around the kitchen, looking for something to do that would require little effort and less thought. 'Dad's put up one of his notices again.'

Mum sighed. 'Oh dear! What's this one about?'

'Using the toilets properly.'

'First Miss Dawn, then your father. Why is everyone fixated on their nether regions today?' Mum frowned.

'Don't ask me. D'you want some help?'

'No, I've got it all under control,' Mum said hastily. 'No offence, love, but you helping out in the kitchen is like a bull helping out in a crystal glass shop!'

'Well, thank you very much. And when I don't offer —' Nova got no further.

Jude and Jake raced into the kitchen, crashing into her. 'Ow! Can't you two watch where you're going?' she stormed at them.

Only seconds behind them sprinted Rainbow, Nova's older sister. 'Mum, tell those little nappy squirts to stay out of my room or I'll . . . I'll torture them,' she raged, snatching at her brothers.

Jake and Jude ducked under and around the table, trying to keep out of reach of both Rainbow and Nova. The twins hid behind Mum as Rainbow did her best to grab first one, then the other, without much success.

'Raye, calm down. Nova, they bashed into you by accident so back off. OK, you two, what've you been up to?' Mum had to sidestep, then front-step to keep between Rainbow and the twins. It looked as if she were line-dancing.

'They've been in my room, searching through my things – that's what they've been doing,' Rainbow fumed. 'Mum, I want a lock on my door and if you don't get someone to do it, I'll do it myself.'

'Jude, is that true? Were you two searching through Raye's bedroom?'

'Only a little bit, Mum,' Jude admitted.

'In a pig's eye!' Raye exploded. 'They've been through all my stuff and my room's a mess.'

'How can you tell?' Mum wasn't trying to be sarcastic.

At least, Nova didn't think she was. From the instantly apologetic look on Mum's face, it'd obviously just slipped out. But it'd slipped out far enough for Rainbow to hear. Rainbow glared at Mum before she turned and marched out of the kitchen.

Mum turned to the twins. 'Could you two please, *please* stay out of Rainbow's room for the sake of my blood pressure? Not to mention my sanity!'

The twins grinned at her. 'At least we give Rainbow something else to worry about apart from boys!' said Jude.

'So what did you get this time?' Nova said eagerly. 'Anything interesting?'

'Raye's writing poems,' Jake informed her solemnly.

'No! Did you manage to get one?'

Jake lifted up his jumper and a piece of paper immediately fluttered out and onto the floor.

'Let's see.' Nova bent to snatch at it but Jake got there first.

'We'll read it,' he told her.

'I wouldn't do that if I were you,' Mum warned. 'It doesn't belong to you and if Raye finds out you've got it, you're on your own!'

'She won't find out, Mum. Don't worry. Ready, Jake?' said Jude.

'Ready, Jude,' Jake replied.

'I really, *really* don't recommend this,' Mum began.

'Never mind her. Read it,' Nova ordered, her eyes ablaze with possibilities.

'I want nothing to do with this.' Mum went back to rolling out her pastry.

'You start, Jake,' said Jude. 'We'll take half each.'

Jake grinned at Nova, then he began, 'Raye's poem:

'I'm a lanky, tall girl
With a cellulite body.
I've got a bulging stomach,
And my bum's big like a lorry.

I've got biceps like a boxer
I've canoes instead of feet,
And when I fart – look out!
'Cos my bottom isn't sweet!'

'Well, that bit is certainly true.' Jude nodded vigorously as he handed over the sheet of paper to his twin.

'My parents are as mad as loons,
My sister's a real pain.
My brothers are the worst of all
They're driving me insane.

What gives me inspiration as
My life heads down the tubes?
The two things that I wouldn't change,
My colour and my —'

'Give me that.' Mum snatched the poem from Jude before he could protest. She glanced down at the writing on the page. 'Oh, dear! Is that really how Raye sees herself?'

'What's she talking about – her bum's big like a lorry!?' Nova scoffed. 'She's thin as a pin. Any skinnier and I'd be able to pick my teeth with her.'

'Why on earth would she think her dad and I are mad? I'm the sanest person I know!' said Mum.

'Mum, you talk to your pastry and Dad is always hanging up peculiar notices for the guests. If that's not barmy, then what is?' said Nova.

'You're a pain! You're a pain!' said Jake to Nova gleefully.

'And we're driving her insane,' said Jude with equal delight. 'Yes!'

Jude and Jake gave each other a high five as a salute to a job well done.

'Look, you two,' said Mum urgently, 'I don't want Raye finding out that you snaffled one of her poems, d'you hear? She's going through enough as it is.'

'What's she going through then?' Nova asked.

'She's a teenager,' Mum replied. As far as she was concerned that explained everything.

'I can't wait to be a teenager if it means I'll get away with all the stuff Raye does,' said Nova.

'You've always been stroppy, Nova, so your dad and I have had a lot of practice in dealing with you. Your sister, however, is different.'

'Thanks a lot!' Nova stormed.

'I didn't mean it like that!' Mum amended quickly. 'I just —'

'What does stroppy mean?' asked Jude.

'Awkward, stubborn, difficult — basically a pain in the neck,' Nova supplied.

'I just meant —' said Mum desperately.

'Save it, Mum!' Nova flounced over to the fridge.

Mum raised her eyes heavenwards.

'Are we going to be like that when we become teenagers?' Jake asked hopefully.

'Yeah, are we?' added Jude, with equal alacrity.

'Over my dead body,' Mum told them at once.

'How come the girls get to do it and we don't?' Jake pouted.

'Yeah, how come?' Jude added.

Mum said in a long-suffering voice, 'Why do I have the

sudden urge to bake enough bread to feed every mouth in the country?' She turned back to Rainbow's poem, the crease between her eyebrows deepening.

Jude and Jake grinned at each other. Mum was now softened up nicely!

'Mum, can we go and play in the attic?' Jake asked casually.

'Not in my bedroom,' Nova said quickly. Half the attic space had been converted into her bedroom and she guarded her space ferociously. The other half was used for storage and contained old-fashioned trunks and dusty boxes and piles of papers that only Jude and Jake enjoyed going through.

'Yeah, can we?' asked Jude.

'Can you what?' asked Mum, preoccupied.

'Play in the attic.'

'OK,' said Mum.

Stunned, Nova stared at her. Mum's brain obviously wasn't switched on. As the twins turned to run out of the room, Mum suddenly realized what she'd been asked. She moved at greased lightning speed to grab both of them by the arm.

'Just a minute, you two. No dropping water bombs on the heads of the guests, no dust sheets over your heads and pretending to be ghosts, no strange noises, no banana skins, no itching powder, no fake dog poo, no real cockroaches, no stink bombs, no worms in any of the beds, no fart alarms, no frogs in any of the baths. NO NONSENSE. Is that understood?'

'Ma'am, yes, ma'am!' Jude and Jake saluted in unison.

'I mean it. If I hear from any of the guests that you two have been up to your usual antics, you're both in BIG trouble.'

'We heard,' Jake sniffed.

'No need to go on and on,' Jude added, dusting the flour off his arm.

They both ran off with Mum eyeing them suspiciously. She directed a worried look at Nova.

'Don't worry, Mum,' Nova said. 'Between me, Raye, Dad and the other guests, they probably won't get away with too much. Probably.'

'That makes me feel a whole heap better,' Mum replied dryly.

Nova grinned at her.

Dad burst through the door. 'Karmah, has Mr Jackman deigned to tell you how long he's staying with us?' he asked.

'No, he hasn't. And as long as we have his credit card details, he can dither as long as he likes,' Mum replied.

Nova wondered if she had time to slide out, tear down Dad's latest notice and duck out of sight for an hour or so until he calmed down. It was worth a try. Edging behind him, she started to sidestep silently towards the door.

'I'm not happy with guests not letting me know how long they plan to stay. How am I meant to schedule in future bookings if I don't know when the guests are going to leave?' Dad complained, adding without turning round, 'Nova, for the last time, leave my notice alone. D'you hear?'

'What future bookings?' Nova piped up from behind him, peeved.

Mum glared at Nova, her expression piercing. Nova knew exactly what that look meant. They'd been at the hotel for almost two years now and Dad had tried just about everything to make Phoenix Manor more popular, but nothing really took off. The hotel was set high up on the gently sloping St Bart's Head, overlooking St Bart's Bay. To the front of the hotel there were stunning views across the bay to the sea beyond. The formal gardens behind the hotel merged into Siren's Copse. Underground tunnels criss-crossed the land for miles around – tunnels where, centuries before, smugglers were rumoured to have brought silks and brandy ashore from continental Europe, using the secret underground passages to hide from the authorities. There was meant to be a tunnel entrance hidden in the bay somewhere and another one in Siren's Copse, but no one had ever found them. In a setting steeped in local history, the hotel should've been a dead certainty for success – but it wasn't. Business was slow, not to mention a constant worry. And as Mum pointed out, Dad didn't need his family constantly moaning on and making him feel like a failure.

'We do all right, Nova,' Mum said, an edge to her voice.

'Yeah, right.' Nova headed for the fridge. 'I'm thirsty. Any juice or something fizzy in there?'

'Nova Alexandra Clibbens, don't even think about it!' said Mum as Nova raised the orange juice carton to her lips. 'Use a glass.'

'What's that?' Dad pointed to the piece of paper, now covered in flour, beside Mum's pastry.

Mum picked it up. 'Oh, that's —'

Raye marched into the room. 'Mum, I want you to — Is that one of my poems?'

Nova wasn't surprised that Raye had spotted it. Her sister always did have eyes like a hawk.

'Yes, but I . . .' Mum spluttered.

'Mum, how could you? My poems are private and personal.' Raye snatched it out of her mother's hand, directing a look at her that would've had a weaker person gasping for breath. 'You're worse than the twins.'

'So what's so good about your boobs that you wouldn't change them?' Nova couldn't resist asking.

'Mum, I can't believe you! You let Nova read it?' Raye asked, scandalized.

'Why d'you want to change your boobs, Rainbow?' asked Dad, getting hold of entirely the wrong end of the stick. 'I hope you're not thinking of plastic surgery or some other such nonsense at your age.'

'Leave my boobs out of this,' Raye said furiously, her beige cheeks now fiery red.

'Raye wants to have her boobs done,' Nova sang.

'I do not!'

'Raye wants to have her boobs done!'

Raye used sign language to tell Nova exactly where to go and what to do when she got there.

'Rainbow, that's quite enough of that,' Dad admonished.

After glaring at Dad and scowling at Nova, Rainbow turned her attention to Mum. 'I'm not going to forget this in a hurry,' she snapped. 'Thanks a lot for showing me up in front of everyone.'

'Now wait just a minute . . .' Mum said, once she'd scraped her jaw off the floor.

But she was talking to the closing kitchen door. Rainbow was long gone! The kitchen was stony silent as Mum turned to see Dad and Nova watching her. Nova drank her orange juice, looking away so she wouldn't be blamed for what had just happened. Dad moved in to stand behind Mum.

'What you need is a stress-relieving massage,' he said, his fingers already digging into Mum's shoulders.

Mum winced and tried to pull away, but nothing doing. Nova felt sorry for her. She had already experienced Dad's massages at a time when she used to suffer from leg cramps. The cramps were less painful! Mum tried again to shrug out of his grasp, but Dad just held on tighter.

'Ah!' There was no mistaking the satisfaction in Dad's voice. 'Isn't that much better? Let's just work out those kinks.'

'The kinks are all gone,' Mum said hastily, trying to pull herself away. 'Let go, dear. I'm getting pins and needles up and down my arms.'

'Nonsense. Five minutes of one of my massages and you'll be smiling for the rest of the week.'

By which time, Mum had had enough. She raised her hands to prise Dad's fingers off her protesting muscles, starting with his little fingers first. 'Tyler, back off! I'm not being funny but your massages are hellish!'

Dad's hands dropped to his sides. 'Pardon?'

'Every time you give me a massage, it feels like a golden eagle has landed on me and is trying to tear off bits of my body.' Mum rubbed at each of her sore shoulders in turn.

'I see,' Dad said with icy politeness.

Nova raised her eyebrows. Today obviously wasn't Mum's day for tact, but Nova could see she was still trying to work through the pain in her shoulders as she spoke!

'If that's how you feel, I'll take my eagle's talons somewhere else.' Dad stormed out of the kitchen without another word.

Nova fought down a grin. 'Shall I break out the bread dough, Mum?' she asked.

Rubbing her throbbing temples, Mum replied, 'Please!'

4. Liam

I marched down the hallway, grabbing my jacket off the banister on my way to the front door.

'Liam, get back here.'

I kept striding, pulling open the front door. Dad rushed up behind me and pushed it shut, painfully jerking my fingers in the process.

'Liam, you'll do as I say. This is still my house.'

'Your house?' *I scoffed.* 'Mum left it to me. Or are you too drunk to remember that?'

Dad's face went seven shades of red. He looked like one of those DIY paint charts. 'Don't talk to me like that, boy. I'm still your father.' *Spittle flew out of his mouth to land on my cheek.*

'I wish to God I could forget.' *I took a great deal of pleasure in scrubbing at my face with the back of my hand. I let my eyes blaze, making no attempt to hide what I was feeling.* 'Look at you. You'd be a joke if you weren't so pathetic!'

I glared down at Dad, silently daring him to try something. At sixteen, I was several centimetres taller than him and I was glad for every single one of them. Burning spots of pink appeared on Dad's cheeks as his glance slid away. He obviously couldn't take the way I was looking at him. Good!

'I do my best for you, Liam,' *he sighed.* 'I know you don't believe that, but I do.'

'You save your best for the local pub. You've no interest in anything or anyone except yourself.'

'That's not fair —'

'Fair!' *I exploded. I pointed to my brother, who couldn't stop sniffing as he sat on the top stair, taking it all in.* 'Every stitch of clothing on Josh's back was bought by me. If it wasn't for my Saturday job, we'd be walking around in rags.'

'I do my best,' Dad repeated.

'Oh, do me a favour.' I shook my head. 'You have no idea what I want, what I'm doing, nothing. I passed all my mock exams but you weren't even interested enough to ask me how I did.'

'I . . . well done . . .'

'Don't strain yourself, Dad.' My contempt sliced into him with every word. 'The first chance I get, I'm outta here. I'm going to pass my exams and go on to college and, I swear, you will never see me again.'

'Liam, take me with you.' Josh's voice rang out from above us.

'No way. It's time I looked out for myself instead of putting you first all the time. If it wasn't for you, Josh, I'd've left this dump long ago . . .' Josh flinched at my words. I regretted them the moment I said them. Josh's face crumpled. Tears rolled down his face. His nose started to drip again.

'You don't have to worry about your brother. Josh is my responsibility. I'll take care of him,' Dad insisted.

I stared at him. Did he really believe what he was saying? Couldn't he hear himself? My head was full of bitter words which tripped and tumbled over each other in their haste to leave my mouth. There were too many of them, darting back and forth much too fast. They hurt so much they made my eyes sting. I clamped my lips together. Silent moments passed.

'Dad, get out of my way,' I said, when I could trust myself to speak without making a fool of myself.

On the stairs Josh's sniffing was getting louder and more frequent. I glanced up at him, watching with quiet desperation as the tears trickled faster down his cheeks.

'I've got to get out of here.' I could hear the despair in my voice and despised myself for it. Wrenching open the door, I ran from the house, leaving the door open behind me.

31

'Liam, take me with you,' Josh called out from behind me. 'Please, take me with you.'

I ran faster. Ran and ran until my heart roared like a wounded lion. But even the roar couldn't drown out Josh's words.

'Liam, take me with you . . .'

I covered my ears with my hands as I ran.

'Liam, take me with you . . .'

I can't, Josh.

I can't.

5. Rainbow

Rainbow was still steaming. Why couldn't she live with a normal family in a normal house in a normal neighbourhood? Preferably somewhere in a big city where there were actual things to see and do. Instead she was stuck out in the middle of nowhere-by-the-sea with the brothers from hell. After nearly two years Rainbow still missed her old school and her old friends. She was beginning to wonder if she'd ever get used to life in Phoenix Manor. She always felt like she was fifteen minutes ahead of everyone else at the hotel. She just didn't fit, no matter how hard she tried. And the twins weren't helping.

'If I catch those two in my room just once more . . . I swear! And no jury of girls my age would convict,' Rainbow ranted in an undertone. 'I am so fed up with . . . with — Omigod! He's gorgeous!'

Rainbow came to an abrupt, complete halt and stared. The boy standing at the reception desk had her full attention. Those lips! Oh, those kissable lips! And that nose. Strong and masculine. And those eyes! Omigod, those beautiful brown eyes. Like mysterious pools of . . .

'Er, excuse me, love, but d'you know where the staff are? We want to book in,' said a man's voice from far away.

'Sorry?' Rainbow had to drag her gaze away from the angel in front of her. A short, reasonable-looking man and a slightly taller, sour-faced blonde woman stood behind the Boy Wonder. The man had brown hair flecked with abundant silver strands and wore a genuinely amused smile on his face. The woman next to him didn't though. She was not so much frowning as scowling at Rainbow.

'D'you know where the staff are?' the man repeated.

'I'll book you in. That's no trouble.' Rainbow immediately moved behind the reception desk. No way was she letting Mr Snog-Me-Until-I'm-Breathless out of her sight until she had his name, age, mobile phone number and star sign.

'D'you work here then?' the man asked dubiously.

'My family runs this hotel,' Rainbow informed him, with false modesty. This was one of those rare occasions when she actually volunteered the information.

'And those are your room rates?' He pointed to the sign behind her.

Rainbow nodded. What did he expect to find under a huge sign with the heading ROOM RATES? Second-hand car prices?

'We're Mr and Mrs Stanley and this is our son, Andrew. We booked a room a fortnight ago. Does the family room come with a double and a single bed or three singles?'

Rainbow stopped listening after she'd heard the hunk's name. 'Hi, Andrew.' She turned on what she hoped was a casual yet friendly smile. Not too forward, but not too reluctant. Not too eager, yet not too formal. A genuine smile from the eyes. With just a hint of mystery and a dash of promise.

'Hi. Good to meet you. What's your name?' Andrew asked. And his voice was deep and flowed like honey. Wow! Gorgeous all over.

And then Rainbow realized what he'd asked her. Her heart sank. 'My name? My name is . . . er . . . Raye . . . All my friends call me Raye. You can call me Raye too if you like.'

'Excuse me, but d'you think we could book in some time before the end of the century?' his mum cut in.

Rainbow glared at her. How rude! 'Could you fill in

this registration form, please?' She handed Mrs Stanley the form with a painted-on smile, then turned back to Mr Tall, Dark and Drool-Slobber Handsome. 'Will you be here for long?'

Please! Please!

'Two days. We leave on Sunday,' Andrew replied.

Yes!

'Well, I hope you have a pleasant stay. If there's anything you need, anything at all . . .'

'Thanks, Rainbow. I'll take over now.' Dad practically pushed her to one side as he smiled at the new guests.

'Rainbow?' Andrew raised his eyebrows.

Rainbow's face immediately began to radiate heat. She could've died. 'My dad's idea,' she informed him quickly. 'I hate it.'

'I don't,' said Andrew. 'It's original. Unusual. It suits you.'

'D'you think so?'

Andrew nodded. And for the first time since Rainbow was about seven, she didn't mind her name.

'We'd like a family room,' said Mr Stanley. 'I was asking your daughter if your family rooms come with a double and a single bed or three singles?'

'A double bed and one single,' Dad replied. 'But as we're not too busy at the moment, I can let you have a double room with an adjoining single for the same price, if you'd like?'

'My own room. Great! Perfect,' Andrew enthused.

'I'm not sure about that . . .' Mrs Stanley began.

'Mum, I'm perfectly old enough to stay in a room of my own. I'll behave,' Andrew said silkily. 'I promise.'

A strange feeling came over Rainbow as she watched Andrew and his parents regard each other. There was something going on, some strange undercurrent that Andrew's words had provoked.

'That's OK then. I'm very keen on guests who behave themselves!' Dad laughed.

And just like that, the tension in the air vanished. Rainbow wondered if maybe she'd imagined it. She wasn't sure. But she didn't think so.

'Rainbow, could you . . .? Rainbow?' Dad prodded his daughter's arm to get her attention.

'What?'

'If you can stop fluttering your eyelashes for five seconds, could you get me the keys to the Dickens and the Austen rooms please?'

Rainbow's cheeks began to burn – badly. Honestly! She could've kicked Dad in the shins. 'I am not fluttering my eyelashes,' she hissed, before turning to get the keys.

'Dickens room?' Mr Stanley asked.

'All our rooms are named after famous writers. Dead ones. I don't want to be sued. It was my idea actually. It came to me about a week after we took over this place and the minute I thought of it, I said to myself, "Tyler, the job's a good 'un!" And fortunately my wife agreed. You'll meet her later. Her name is Karmah. She's in the kitchen at the moment — Ow! Rainbow!'

'Here are your keys.' Rainbow thrust them into Mr Stanley's hand. She'd had to step on Dad's foot in the process to get him to shut up. He was burbling on like talking had just come into fashion.

'Will you be dining here tonight? My wife is a great cook,' Dad smiled.

Rainbow stared at him. How could he just open his mouth and lie like that?

'Er, I don't —' began Mrs Stanley.

'Go on, Mum,' Andrew interrupted. 'I'm a bit tired. I'd like to stay in this evening.'

'Tired? Are you sure you're OK?' His mum was all flustered concern. 'Is there anything I can do?'

'No, Mum. Stop flapping.' Andrew smiled to take the sting out of his words.

Rainbow was not impressed with Mrs Stanley.

'OK.' Mrs Stanley turned back to Dad. 'Can we book a table for eight o'clock, please?'

'Certainly. I'll make a note of that. The dining room is just through those double doors,' said Dad, pointing past reception to his right.

'And we'll need a table for three for eight tomorrow,' Mrs Stanley added.

'Pardon?'

'For three people, for eight o'clock tomorrow night,' Mrs Stanley explained impatiently.

She was getting right up Rainbow's nose and no mistake.

'It's Andrew's birthday tomorrow,' said Mr Stanley, smiling apologetically at Rainbow and her dad.

'How old will you be?' Rainbow asked Andrew directly.

'Sixteen,' he replied with a smile.

'Just a year older than me.'

'You look older.'

'Thanks.' Rainbow couldn't believe how he always knew exactly the right things to say. It was uncanny.

'Maybe it would be better if we went elsewhere,' said Mrs Stanley, glancing frostily at Rainbow before turning back to Rainbow's dad. 'Can you recommend a good restaurant?'

Before Dad could say a word, Andrew got in first. 'No, Mum. I want my birthday dinner here. This is just fine.'

'You're sure?' Mrs Stanley asked doubtfully.

'Positive. And it is *my* birthday.'

'If you insist.' Mrs Stanley shrugged.

Andrew winked at Rainbow, who smiled back. His mum was a gorgon but he more than made up for her.

'D'you need help with your bags?' Dad asked hopefully.

They might have thought he was going out of his way to help them, but Rainbow knew the hope in his voice was because he was praying not to have to carry their luggage. Dad had a bad back and lifting heavy suitcases was not what the doctor ordered.

'No thanks. We can manage.' Andrew spoke before his parents could. 'Raye, will you be eating at eight too?'

I am now. 'I might be,' Rainbow smiled. After all, it didn't pay to seem too, *too* eager.

'Hope to see you later then,' said Andrew. He and his parents headed up the stairs.

Count on it, Rainbow thought. Even if she had to drag him to the dining room by his hair roots, they'd meet up again later.

'Ah! Young love!' Dad sighed.

The sigh quickly changed into a cough when Rainbow turned the full force of her outraged glare at him.

'Something wrong, darling?' Dad asked, his face all innocence.

Rainbow marched off without deigning to answer.

'Something I said, Raye?' Dad laughed after her.

Rainbow kept on walking. And not once, not once did she realize she was being watched.

6. Nova and Miss Eve

Nova sighed, the way she always did when she thought about her sister. Less than a couple of years ago they'd been so close. What'd happened since then? It would've been so fantastic to go to the beach or go shopping or just hang out together in the hotel. But nothing doing. Over the past year or so Raye had backed right away from doing anything with Nova. She didn't even want to be seen with her. Not in the hotel. Not at school. Nowhere. No way!

'Nova, stop swinging on the banister!' Dad called out from the reception desk.

Nova carried on rocking to and fro, her hands wrapped around the bottom banister post. Nova the pain. That was her new name. So now Raye was too old to hang out with and the twins were too young. The half-term break was dragging more than usual this time round. Nova usually longed for school holidays and they ended much too soon – but this time not much had been going on at the hotel. Friday morning and nothing dawning.

'Nova, am I talking Martian? Get off the banister,' said Dad.

Nova sighed again, but did as she was told this time. She thought for a moment. The gardens. She'd go for a long walk across the gardens and after that maybe down to the beach. She headed across the hall towards the front door.

Miss Eve emerged from the hotel lounge. 'Ah, Nova, my poppet. How are you today?'

Nova bristled with indignation. How many times did

she have to repeat herself before Miss Eve got it? 'Poppet' was out, OUT, OUT!

'Fine,' Nova muttered in a voice that suggested she was anything but.

'I wonder if I might have a word?' Miss Eve continued.

'Any word in particular?'

'Pardon?'

'Nothing,' Nova replied hastily. She didn't want to spend the next ten minutes explaining. She looked at Miss Eve but her glance quickly slid away again. There was something about the elderly woman that set the hairs at the back of Nova's neck bristling. Miss Eve had off-white, blue-rinsed hair which matched her pale blue eyes. Ice-cold eyes, Nova always thought. She was tall and straight and laughed a lot, but very rarely smiled. Miss Dawn was the opposite: she smiled a lot but very rarely laughed. Miss Dawn seemed the sadder of the two.

'Where're you off to?' asked Miss Eve.

'I was going to take a walk in the garden. A long walk.' Nova hoped that would put the old dear off. 'A long, long walk.'

'Excellent! I was just thinking of doing the same thing myself. Let's walk together, poppet,' suggested Miss Eve.

Nova's heart and hopes sank. She had wanted to spend some time by herself, not spend the next half hour listening to Miss Eve rabbit on about her various aches and pains and varicose veins. 'Are you sure you're up to it, Miss Eve?' Nova couldn't give up without a fight. 'I'll be walking quite quickly.'

'My dear poppet, I have more stamina than you might think.' Miss Eve's eyes twinkled wickedly. 'Why, if I were to tell you some of the things I've got up to in my time—'

'Please don't,' Nova interrupted. 'I mean, please don't

bother yourself. You should save your energy. For the walk.'

'Of course. Shall we go then?'

'Maybe you should go and get a cardie? It looks a bit nippy out there.' Brilliant! Nova congratulated herself on her ploy. While Miss Eve was off getting herself a cardigan, Nova would be out of there faster than a rat up a drainpipe. Perfect!

'No thanks. I'm just fine,' replied Miss Eve. She linked arms with Nova and set a brisk pace for the door. 'Don't dawdle, poppet. As you quite rightly said, it's not a proper walk if it's not bracing.'

Nova turned her head, searching for something, some-one, *anyone* to rescue her. But there was only Dad at the reception desk. Nova threw him her best beseeching look, mouthing, 'Help!' in the process.

'Enjoy!' Dad called out, grinning maliciously as he waved goodbye.

Nova was sink, sank, sunk – without a trace. She glared at Dad as Miss Eve continued to drag her out the front door.

Miss Eve stood on the top step looking around at the autumn countryside. Nova looked around as well. She never got tired of this view. The front of the hotel stood tall and still like a faithful sentinel. It was set back about two hundred metres from the cliff edge but was impressive enough to be seen from boats heading in and out of St Bart's Bay. In past times fishermen in their vessels had been the ones to admire or envy the Manor House, as it had been called. Now leisure boats and small yachts sailed out, not even giving Phoenix Manor a backwards glance. At the back of the hotel were the hotel grounds, over an acre of formally landscaped gardens. But the best thing of all was that from the front step, no matter what the weather, you could see or hear or taste the sea. Nova loved the way the sea shone like a shattered mirror when it was calm or rose up in a fury in stormy weather. Sometimes she went down to the cliff edge and leaned against the wall overlooking the bay and just watched the sea for hours on end. And sometimes she almost believed that the sea lay there watching her as well.

Nova remembered how she'd complained incessantly about moving away from her school and her friends. She'd been worse than Rainbow and that was saying something – until she'd stood on this top step and savoured the view. And with the view, all thoughts of her previous life had faded to a place where they didn't hurt any more.

Nova inhaled deeply, her eyes closed as she drank in the salty tang in the air. Next to her Miss Eve did the same, only to start coughing almost immediately.

'Ah, smell that fresh sea air. Doesn't it make you feel sick?' asked Miss Eve. 'Doesn't it make you long for car fumes mixed with the gentle waft of stale burgers and backed-up, overflowing sewers?'

'Did you originally live in a city then?' Nova asked to be polite.

'Oh, I've lived everywhere, poppet. Miss Dawn and me, we like to travel.' Miss Eve laughed like a woman possessed, though for the life of her, Nova couldn't see what was so funny.

'Private joke, poppet. Private joke,' Miss Eve supplied when she saw the way Nova was looking at her.

She tugged Nova down the stairs. They turned left to walk round the side of the hotel to the gardens at the back. Miss Eve was striding along as if she were on a route march. Nova had to trot beside her to keep up.

'You said you wanted to talk to me?' Nova gasped.

'Oh, yes. Nothing terribly important. I just wondered

whether Miss Dawn had spoken to you recently?' Miss Eve asked lightly.

'Yeah. Earlier today.' Where had those tiny beads of sweat prickling her forehead come from? Was it just the fast walk or something else? What was it about this woman . . .?

'What did she say?' asked Miss Eve.

'Good morning.'

'Good morning to you too, my poppet. But what did Miss Dawn say to you?'

'She said, "Good morning",' Nova explained patiently.

'Anything else?'

'Like what?' Nova asked, curious now in spite of herself. The beads of sweat still kept coming, even though it wasn't that warm and Nova wasn't trotting that quickly any more. It was as if every cell in her body was on alert.

'Did she mention any of the other guests at all?' asked Miss Eve.

Nova stopped trotting altogether and pulled away. Miss Eve turned with a ready smile on her lips. 'I just wondered, that's all.'

'I can't remember.' Nova frowned. 'I think she said something about Dad falling over the reception desk but not much more than that. Why?'

'As I said, I'm just curious.'

'Why would she mention any of the guests to me?' asked Nova.

'No reason.' Miss Eve started walking again.

Nova's suspicions were well and truly aroused. What was this all about? What was Miss Eve after? Why all the questions and the interest in what Miss Dawn might have said about any of the guests? Miss Eve turned as if she felt Nova studying her. Nova forced herself to smile and walked to catch up.

'When you get to my age, my poppet, poking your nose into other people's business is one of the few pleasures left in life!' said Miss Eve.

Nova nodded, then shrugged.

Miss Eve glanced down at her watch. 'Oh, silly me!' she continued. 'I've got some letters which I need to finish off if they're going to catch the next post. D'you mind if I cut short our walk, poppet?'

'No! I mean, that's fine,' Nova said in all seriousness.

'We'll have a nice long walk and talk some time soon,' Miss Eve smiled. 'OK?'

'OK,' agreed Nova, thinking, Like when my toes learn to chew gum!

She watched as Miss Eve walked back towards the front of the house. Talk about a lucky escape! There was definitely something about Miss Eve ... Something that made Nova careful of every word she said, and every move she made. Once Miss Eve had rounded the corner of the hotel and was out of sight, Nova turned away, breathing a huge sigh of relief – only to walk straight into someone's chest.

'Ow!' Nova stepped back but it didn't stop her from falling backwards to land on the gravelly path with a thump.

The teenage boy she'd just bumped into stared at her in stunned amazement. His mid-brown eyes were wide with shock. He had short, dark hair and the creases around his mouth indicated either a ready smile or a ready frown – Nova wasn't quite sure which.

'Why don't you look where you're going?' she demanded furiously.

'Why don't you?' the boy replied.

'Because this is my hotel,' Nova said stiffly.

'That shouldn't stop you from looking where you're

going,' said the boy. 'And anyway, I live here too.'

'No. You might be staying here, but this is my home.' Nova tried to scramble to her feet.

The boy put out a hand to help her up. Nova reached out to take it but before she could grab hold, he withdrew it sharply. Nova's bum bounced off the stony ground again.

'Sorry,' said the boy, his hands behind his back.

Nova scowled at him, her eyes ablaze.

'Jeez! If looks could kill . . .' And the boy started laughing.

'You moron!' Nova jumped up. 'I bet your shoe size is bigger than your IQ.'

'It's not, actually. My IQ puts me in the genius category. I've been tested.'

'If you're a genius, I'm the Queen of Sheba,' Nova scoffed.

'Your majesty!' said the boy, bowing slightly.

'When you've quite finished.' This boy was getting more and more irritating. The longer Nova was around him, the more she longed to be somewhere else. She didn't care if she never saw this idiot again. 'Excuse me.' She tried to go round the boy, but he stepped in front of her, blocking her path. To her surprise, he waved his hand in front of her face.

'What's your problem?' Nova asked, eyeing him suspiciously.

'What do I look like?'

Nova stared. 'Pardon?'

'What colour's my hair?'

Nova began to feel just a little bit anxious. This boy definitely had more than one screw loose. Best to humour him. 'Black.' Nova looked closer. 'No. Dark brown.'

The boy took a step forward. Nova took a step back.

'What colour are my eyes?'

'I dunno.' Nova leaned forward for a better look, only to pull back immediately. 'Brown.'

'How tall am I?' The question was fired at Nova.

'What is this? Don't you know what you look like?'

'Just checking.' The boy suddenly grinned from ear to ear.

A couple of eggs short of the full hotel breakfast and no mistake, Nova amended silently. 'Excuse me, I have things to do.' She turned and walked quickly back the way she had come, towards the front of the hotel.

'Wait. I want to talk to you.'

Nova kept walking. She most certainly didn't want to talk to that weirdo. What was it about her that had all the nutters for miles around flocking to her? Maybe she should try a different soap! What was he doing? Watching her leave? Nova turned round. The boy had vanished. Startled, she looked around. He couldn't have reached the other side of the hotel already, not without running – and if he'd run then Nova would've heard his footsteps crunching on the gravel path. And he hadn't cut across the gardens, otherwise he'd still be in sight. Not even an Olympic gold medallist could sprint out of sight that fast.

Nova took another look around. Nothing. Seriously spooked, she quickened her pace as she headed back to the front entrance. Only when she was back inside the hotel did she dare to breathe a sigh of relief. Who was that creep? With a little luck she'd never have to see him again. There was something about him that put her on edge. Mind you, he wasn't bad looking. But that was the only thing he had going for him.

'Dad, who's the boy with — ?' Nova was heading for the reception desk, but then she stopped abruptly.

Weirdo was back and standing right next to Dad behind the reception desk. He was peering over Dad's shoulder, but at the sound of Nova's voice he looked up and waved.

'What're you doing behind there? Come out!' Nova demanded furiously.

'Huh? I work here.' Dad frowned.

'Not you, Dad. How did you get back in here before me?' Nova asked the boy.

'I never left,' Dad replied, bewildered.

'Not you, Dad. *Him*.'

Dad looked round. 'Nova, who're you talking to?'

'I thought guests weren't allowed behind the reception desk?'

'They're not.' Dad's frown deepened.

'Then tell him to move.'

'Tell who?'

'Him,' Nova said impatiently, pointing at the boy, who now had a beaming smirk on his face.

Dad turned in the direction of Nova's pointing finger. 'Nova, there's no one here except you and me.'

'Dad, this isn't the time for a wind-up.'

'My feelings exactly. Go and wind up your mother instead,' Dad huffed.

'Why did you let him behind the desk?' Nova asked, exasperated.

'Who?'

Nova was just about to explode when Weirdo put his finger up to his lips. The gesture momentarily took the wind out of Nova's sails – but only momentarily.

'Dad —' She got no further.

Weirdo walked right *through* Dad and the reception desk to stand in front of Nova. 'I wouldn't bother if I were you,' he said. 'It seems that you're the only one in this dump who can see me. Hi, I'm Liam.' And he held out his hand.

Two seconds maximum of stunned silence, then Nova opened her mouth – and screamed blue murder!

Liam grimaced and stuck his fingers in his ears. Nova screamed until her throat felt like it was on fire, but even then she didn't stop.

Dad ran out from behind the reception desk. 'Nova? Nova, stop it. What's the matter? Nova, talk to me.'

Mum ran in from the kitchen. 'What's happened? What on earth is going on?'

'I thought you of all people would take it better than that!' Liam shouted above the din, fading out to disappear altogether.

Nova's head was spinning and she felt sick. Was she going to faint? Was this what it was like to be on the verge of fainting? Her heart was trembling and her blood was racing and everything around her was moving in and out of her vision like a telly moving back and forth on roller skates. Nova took a deep breath, then another, still staring into the space where Liam had just been.

'Nova, what's wrong?' Dad repeated frantically.

Hotel guests appeared on the stairs and from the hotel lounge.

'Nova?'

Her heartbeat began to slow down from frenzied to merely frantic. Her mum and dad stood in front of her, anxiety and concern written all over their faces.

'Nova, darling, what is it?' Mum said urgently.

'Nova, talk to us. What's wrong?' Dad pleaded.

'He's . . . he's a ghost!' said Nova at last. 'Dad, there was a ghost standing behind you and he walked right through you!'

Dad straightened up, his expression incredulous. 'You saw a what?' he repeated. 'A ghost?'

The other guests looked at each other, startled. Mrs Stanley drew her cardigan closer to her, looking around anxiously.

'You saw no such thing,' Mum warned Nova sternly.

'But, Mum, I —'

'Nova, your joke has gone far enough. You're frightening the guests — OK?'

Nova looked round. The guests were all peering at her. A couple of them looked amused; Mrs Stanley and most of the others didn't.

'I'm sorry, Mum. It wasn't really a ghost. It . . . it was a spider — above Dad's head.'

The guests melted away with disapproving shakes of their heads or sympathetic smiles. Mum's look of incredulity melted into something else. Nova knew she was in trouble.

'It was an enormous spider. It was the spider from hell!' Nova tried to defend herself.

'Go to your room,' Mum said furiously. '*Now!*'

Nova set off up the stairs, muttering to herself. Well, what was she supposed to say?

'That is your daughter!' Mum and Dad spoke in unison, pointing at each other in a very accusatory manner.

'If you must know,' Nova called out from the top of the stairs. 'I didn't see a spider. I really did see a ghost!'

'Enough nonsense,' Mum snapped. 'Go to your room.'

'Nova, do as you're told,' Dad ordered. 'You're in enough trouble already, without adding to it.'

Nova's attic bedroom was up another flight of stairs but she ran all the way. She paused outside her bedroom door, puffing and desperately trying to gulp down air to catch her breath. The boy she'd seen — the *ghost* she'd seen — was he real or was she still asleep and dreaming the whole thing or was she imagining things? Nova dismissed the last two options. She never imagined things, well, hardly ever. And she'd seen the boy – what did he say his name was? Liam? Well, she'd seen him as large as life. *Hadn't she?* With a sigh, Nova opened her bedroom door – and gasped. There, sitting on her bed, was Liam.

7. Liam

I walked and walked. Down by the sea front. Along the pier. Back past the railway station. Through Jubilee Park. Just walking, trying to outdistance my thoughts. I kept hearing Josh say 'Take me with you.' I couldn't get his words out of my head. They played like an undying echo.

'Take me with you . . .'

Why, Josh? So you can end up a loser like me? And the worst thing of all was, I knew I was throwing my life away. I was angry all the time, resentful all the time. All I wanted to do was hit out, hit back, at school, at home – it didn't really matter where. That's why I had to get away – before I choked on all the feelings inside me. Josh would be OK. He'd survive. Besides, Josh is the brains of the family. The obvious brains! Good school reports. Good test results.

'Josh is very intelligent . . .'

'Josh is a pleasure to teach . . .'

'Josh has a keen interest in the subject . . .'

He'd never had a bad report in his life. And it didn't take a genius to figure out what all those school reports were really saying.

'Josh isn't like his older brother . . .'

No, he isn't. He hasn't a clue how to look after himself. I've always done it for him. I've done nothing else but look after Josh since Mum died. Just call me Polyfilla – filling all the gaps in Josh's life so he wouldn't miss Mum as much as I did.

Do.

My brother is the artistic one, the sensitive one, the articulate one. Me? I'm Conan the Barbarian compared to him. I know that's how I'm considered. And you know what, I don't care. I can look after myself. No one ever asked me to be artistic or poetic. A couple of silly pranks at school and that was it – my card was marked. They were never going to give me a chance after that. Never in a million years. I was even sent for a test – what they called a psychological evaluation. Dad hit the roof, of course. Until it became clear that I wasn't a moron, or even average. The tests showed I had a well-above-average IQ. That shocked everyone. Even me, to be honest. I'd spent so long listening to everyone tell me how useless I was that even I'd started to believe it. My IQ rating is the only reason they didn't kick me out of school, I reckon. But after the test, I really let rip. I was untouchable. I was invincible. And some of the things I got up to . . . Silly, hurtful things. Not that I'm making excuses. But taking the test and everyone's reaction to it did something to me. I realized that before the results, nothing was expected from me. No talent, no hard work, no commitment, no brains, no sense, no ambitions – nothing. So I decided that if everyone expected nothing, that was precisely what they were going to get.

I don't walk all over people. But I don't let them walk all over me either.

Poor Josh! Being lumbered with a brother like me. I tease him and wind him up something chronic, and he still adores me. Silly beggar! My friends call him the lapdog – even to his face 'cos of the way he follows me around. I can't change direction without tripping over him first. Josh, the anchor. Josh, the chain. Josh, the lapdog. Josh, the pain. Josh, my brother. Josh, the one thing in this world I really care about.

Sometimes . . . sometimes I feel like I want to just demolish things because there's so much inside me that I want to say and do but I can't get it out. I want to make things, build things. I want to climb. I want to fly. But my brother keeps me tethered to the ground. So I smash things instead.

'Take me with you.'

How can I, when because of you, I never leave? Take you

where? Take you to nowhere. Take you to nothing. You don't need me, Josh. Sooner or later, you'll fly on your own. And I'll be stuck here, down on the ground, watching you fly. And hating you. I don't want to hate you. You're my brother. I care about you.

But I'm afraid. You scare me, Josh.

Where am I?

Jeez! Manor Hotel. Have I really walked that far? Manor Hotel used to be the Manor House, owned a couple of centuries before by Count whoever or Lord someone-or-other. It was converted into a hotel about thirty years ago, though, passing from one person to another, none of whom seemed to want it. The last owner (a woman, I think) closed it down over nine years ago and it has stood empty ever since.

But I love this place. It's derelict and practically falling down, but it's such an excellent place to hang out. Me and my friends used to run riot around here. Breaking windows. Spray painting the walls. Making our mark. It was our hide-out. A home away from home. I haven't been over this way in months though. Who put all this wire-mesh fencing up? It's too high to get over. I'll go round. Hopefully the original wire fence at the back is still there and they haven't replaced it. That was always our way in – the gap in the wire security fence over by the gardens. Gardens! The polite way to put it! They looked more like an overgrown wasteland than anything else. But there's something about this place, set on the sloping cliff top, with the sea before it and the so-called gardens behind. What I didn't tell my mates was that sometimes, when things got really bad at home, I'd come up here by myself and just wander around and explore. It was somewhere to be away from things. To escape. Manor Hotel. I haven't been up here for months. I can't believe I haven't been up here for months. Maybe that's why I feel so stressed.

Oh please! Look at that! What a useless sign! Is that really meant to put anyone off?

WARNING!
THIS SITE IS DANGEROUS. NO
TRESPASSING.

SECURITY GUARDS AND PATROL DOGS
ARE EMPLOYED ON THIS SITE.

TRESPASSERS WILL BE
PROSECUTED.

Yeah right! That sign has been there for the last five years and in all that time, I've never seen a single security guard or dog. Who're they trying to kid? Not that it'd put me off even if there were guards. I really don't want to go home tonight.

How about if I stay here? Just for one night. It'll do Dad good to think I really have gone. And as for Josh . . . he'll survive without me for one night. Just one night. Manor Hotel is a bit of a wreck but I'll find somewhere warm and dry. I know this place like the back of my hand. Don't worry, Josh, I'll see you tomorrow. I just can't face going back home tonight, that's all. One night won't hurt. One night won't hurt anyone.

I'll see you tomorrow, Josh.

8. Rainbow

This sucks!

It's not fair!

What am I going to wear? I need some new clothes. This top is so five minutes ago! I hate my life. Look at the state of my hair. Look at the state of me. I need something to wear for tonight. Something to knock Andrew's eyes out. Something to convince him that I'm the girl of his daydreams. A fantasy girl! Yeah, I like the sound of that. So what should I wear? This may be the back of beyond but that's no reason to go around looking like something the dog dug up − or threw up.

I wonder if I can get Mum or Dad to cough up for a new outfit. Not that I'd get much round here. I'd need to go to the city to get some really decent gear. And that's not going to happen in the next couple of hours, is it? Maybe with some carefully applied make-up I can take the focus off my outfit. I wouldn't have to do any of this if we lived somewhere with a couple of decent clothes shops.

It's not fair.

This sucks!

9. Nova and Liam

'If you're going to scream again, could you warn me first? My ears are still ringing,' said Liam.

A long, long pause.

'Well, aren't you coming in?'

Nova stood right where she was.

'You're not afraid, are you?' Liam asked, amused.

Nova visibly bristled at that. She took a deep breath and walked into the room.

'Are you going to scream again?' asked Liam.

Nova slowly shook her head.

Silence. More silence!

'Are you just going to stare at me all year or will you be speaking some time soon?'

Nova shook her head, then blinked hard. She still couldn't believe it. Here she was, standing in the middle of her bedroom – and there was an actual ghost sitting on her bed. Nova moved forward and waved her left hand in front of Liam's face. She leaned forward and waved her hand right through his head. Jumping back like a scalded cat, she continued to stare at him. Taking another step forward, she waved her hand through Liam's head again. It didn't feel any different to normal air. Slightly cooler perhaps, or maybe that was just her imagination. Nova drank in the sight of Liam. He was really there, wasn't he? She wasn't cracking up, was she? If she was, she'd conjured up a dead good-looking guy. He had the warmest, clearest brown eyes she'd ever seen. He was almost as tall as her dad and that was saying something. Nova waved her hand through his head once more.

'You really *are* a ghost, aren't you?' she whispered. 'A real, live ghost!'

'The pleasure is all yours,' Liam said.

'A real, live ghost in my room,' said Nova. 'What tricks can you do, apart from fading and walking through people, that is? Can you make yourself invisible and move things? Can you change into different animals? Can you shoot fire out of your eyes and fly around the hotel?'

'I'm a ghost, not a mutant X-man.' Liam frowned.

Nova sat down next to him. 'So, is that it then? Can you only fade out and walk through people and objects? Big deal!'

'You were very impressed less than ten minutes ago!' Liam pointed out.

'That was then, and this is now. Well? Can't you do anything else?'

'How about I tell you what you can do instead?'

'All right! All right! Only asking,' said Nova.

But her mind was fired up with possibilities. Liam might just be the answer to a prayer. A hotel with a real, live ghost. Guests would definitely flock to see that – and they'd pay through the nose and ears for it too. OK, so five minutes ago the guests in reception hadn't seemed too keen on the idea of a ghost in the hotel. But Nova hadn't handled that right. If Liam could appear on cue – and disappear, of course – then the guests would know what to expect and wouldn't be afraid. They'd just be . . . thrilled! She'd have to get Liam to appear to her mum and dad. Wait till she told them her plans! Things were definitely looking brighter.

'Hang on! If you're a ghost, how come I bumped into you in the garden?'

Liam turned his head and looked almost embarrassed.

Nova waved her hand through his body again. 'Can you make yourself real any time you like then?'

'I'm already real.' Liam frowned. 'I'm just a ghost, that's all.'

'Why can't I touch you now then?'

'Because, if you must know, Miss Eve stresses me out,' Liam admitted. 'And when I get in a stress, or I get angry or upset I seem to become "real" again — to use your word.'

'Real?'

'Solid. I can touch things and pick up things and others can see me and touch me. But it only lasts for a few minutes at most. And afterwards, I'm totally wiped out.'

'Can Miss Eve see you too?'

'No. At least, I don't think so,' said Liam.

'Why does she stress you out?'

Liam shook his head. 'There's something about her . . .'

'What?'

'I can't explain it. She makes the hairs on the back of my neck stand on end.'

How strange! That was exactly how Nova felt about Miss Eve as well.

'What about Miss Dawn?'

'There's something about her too, but she doesn't freak me out,' Liam admitted. 'At least, not in the same way as Miss Eve.'

'How come Mum and Dad have never seen you?'

'I told you. I can only materialize if I get upset or something.'

'You mean — emotional!' amended Nova.

'I mean upset or something,' Liam corrected briskly. 'And I like to keep myself to myself. Anyway, I don't want your family and the others in this place gawping at me. I'm not some kind of freaky sideshow.'

'No, of course not,' Nova said, hoping he hadn't guessed the plans she'd been busy making in her head. She'd have to pick the right moment to try and persuade him to give her plan a try.

She reached out a tentative finger to prod Liam. Her finger passed straight through him, like moving into the cool space in an empty fridge. 'A real, live ghost!' She drew back her hand, before jabbing it forward once more to prod him. She didn't know what she was expecting. Was she hoping to catch him off guard and find he was solid after all? Nova tried poking him once more.

'Could you stop doing that?'

'Why? You can't feel it.'

'It's still irritating!'

'Are you still feeling stressed then? How come I can still see you?'

'Actually, I was wondering that myself. I'm back to normal now. At least, I feel the way I always feel, so you shouldn't be able to see me,' said Liam, scrutinizing Nova. 'Have you ever seen a ghost before?'

'Not as far as I know,' said Nova.

'You must be more sensitive than most to ghosts. And now you've seen me, it's like you can't stop seeing me – if you see what I mean!'

Nova nodded, adding, 'You could've warned me that you were a ghost. Dad thinks I've lost my marbles.'

'I didn't know you'd freak like that.'

'How did you expect me to react? You walked straight through my dad!'

'It didn't hurt him, did it? So what's the problem?'

'You scared me,' Nova admitted.

'But you're not scared any more, are you?' asked Liam.

Nova considered, then shook her head. Liam looked harmless enough. A bit smarmy and full of himself, but then he was a boy, and a teenage boy at that – so what else was new! But he was strange looking though – mainly because he wasn't strange looking! He didn't float centimetres above the ground or carry his head under his arm. He wasn't dressed in a dazzling white suit, nor was there a glow or an aura around him. In fact, for a ghost he was a bit of a disappointment. He was wearing faded blue jeans and a matching blue-buttoned shirt. His trainers were grubby in places and of an old double-striped design. But even so . . .

'Can I ask you a question?' said Nova.

'Was that it?'

'No.'

'Go on then!'

'I've always wondered something about you ghosts,' Nova said, her brows creased. 'How come you can walk though walls and pass through objects and yet you can still walk on a floor without passing straight through it?'

Liam stared at her in disbelief. 'Because I just can.'

'That's not an answer.'

'It's the only one I can give you,' said Liam. 'It's like asking a bird how come it can fly or a fish how come it can swim. 'Cos it just can – and it's the same with me.'

'Well, that doesn't really explain much,' Nova said, disappointed.

'I can't help that,' Liam said dryly. He sat in silence as Nova regarded him for a long while. 'You'll know me the next time you see me, won't you!' he said at last, clearly irritated.

'How long have you been . . . here?' Nova was going to ask how long he'd been a ghost but somehow it didn't seem quite right. At least, not yet.

'No idea. I think it's been quite a while but it could be a month, could be a year. I don't know.'

'Why not?'

'Time doesn't pass the same way for me as it does for you,' said Liam. 'It goes a lot more slowly.'

'Oh, I see,' said Nova. She didn't really but she let it pass. She sat watching him for a while longer. 'How did you . . . er, come to be here?'

'I had a quarrel with my dad,' said Liam bitterly.

'Pardon?'

'I had a big fight with my dad.'

'And what? You had a heart attack or something?' asked Nova.

'No. Look, I don't want to talk about it.'

'Was it your dad's fault then?'

Liam turned away without answering.

'Sorry. I didn't mean to pry,' said Nova.

'I'll live!' said Liam.

Nova burst out laughing. Liam stared at her. Then he realized what he'd said and smiled. Nova still couldn't believe it. Here she was, chatting to a ghost in her room. She was doing something no one else in her family had ever done. She was the first. A first in itself. 'A real, live ghost . . .' she breathed.

'Yeah, you keep saying that.' Liam frowned. 'I still can't believe you can see me. I've been trolling around this dump *for ever* and no one's ever seen me before.'

'Lucky me!' Nova sniffed. 'And this place is not a dump, thank you very much.'

'I've heard you call it worse.'

'I can 'cos this is my home.'

'It's my home too,' Liam pointed out.

'It's still not a dump,' Nova bristled.

Liam smiled unexpectedly. 'No, it's not. You're right. It used to be, but your family have done a good job.'

'Hmm!' Nova murmured, only slightly placated.

'Sorry. OK?'

'OK,' said Nova reluctantly. 'So why're you here?'

'What d'you mean?' asked Liam.

'Why aren't you in Heaven or Hell or some place where teenage ghosts go? Why're you still here?'

'I don't know.' Liam stood up and walked over to the window. 'You get a good view of the sea from up here.'

Puzzled, Nova was determined not to let the subject drop. 'Do you like it here so much that you don't want to move on?'

'Are you kidding?' Liam rounded on her at once. 'I hate it here.'

'Why don't you leave then?'

'How?'

'I don't know. Just go. Fade out. Disappear. Walk away – or whatever it is that ghosts do.'

Liam turned back to the window. 'I've tried all of those. They don't work.'

Nova considered for a moment. 'You were outside. Why don't you just head off in one direction and keep going?'

At first she thought Liam wasn't going to answer. 'Because the further I go, the darker everything gets. And then I pass out and when I wake up, I'm right back here. And I have no idea how I got back, or who brought me back or how much time has even passed. D'you have any idea what that's like?'

Nova couldn't even begin to imagine what it must be like. She shook her head, but Liam seemed to have forgotten that she was even there. He carried on talking, more to himself than anyone else.

'It's like walking up a long flight of stairs and never, ever getting to the top. Or starting a race and running as hard and as fast as you can and never even getting past the starting line.' Liam's voice was getting softer and softer. 'It's like dying – over and over again, without ever being born.'

And now there was nothing left of him but his voice fading away into nothing. Melting into nowhere.

Nova looked around. 'Liam? Come back. Liam . . .?'

But she was alone.

10. Liam

The sun was low down in the sky now. Another few minutes and it'd set. But there was still enough light to see the Manor Hotel. It was just as I remembered it. Standing in front of it made me feel strange — almost homesick. And heartsick — though I'd never be dibby enough to let anyone know that. How could anyone let the place get into this state? With a bit of TLC it could be halfway decent. The wire-mesh fence might have been reinforced but it still couldn't hide the fact that there was mud and debris and neglect and decay everywhere.

My place.

I mean, where else was I meant to go? I wasn't going home, that's for sure.

The tunnels.

None of my friends knew about the tunnels. Only me. In the cellar of the hotel there were a number of empty, rotting, wooden, floor-to-ceiling wine racks, but behind one of them was a door. I'd only found it by accident when I leaned against one of the stone slabs on an adjacent wall. The door behind one of the wine racks sprang open. It scared the hell out of me at the time and then some. But of course, once I'd got over the shock, I just had to go exploring. I mean, what kind of person would pass up a chance like that? I swung back the wine rack, most of it crumbling to so much dust as soon as I touched it. It was pitch black in there so I only took a few steps inside before I bottled . . . I mean, before I decided to be prudent. After all, I didn't want to break a leg or something.

The next day I came back with a torch, spare batteries and some string so I could do a Theseus and the Minotaur. I spent not just hours, but days exploring those tunnels. Every spare chance I got. They ran back and forth under the hotel and grounds, into the copse on one side and down to a cave set in the cliff by the sea front on the other. Apart from the hidden exit by the sea front, I've only ever found two other exits – but I knew enough to realize that was just the tip of the iceberg. Who knew how many more exits and how many more tunnels ran underground for kilometres around?

I never used the copse tunnel. Too many animals had made it their home over the years and it stank to high heaven, plus I didn't think it'd be too safe with animals burrowing back and forth through it. They didn't seem to venture much beyond the copse though.

The exit I used was in the hotel gardens beneath a hollowed-out slab where some old, weather-worn benches had been dumped. I spent ages clearing them away but it was worth it. Now I could come and go without even entering the hotel building. It was like another world down there. Dry and warm, with a mouldy-earthy smell it didn't take me long to get used to. The tunnels were my favourite part of the Manor Hotel, because I instinctively knew that no one knew about them but me. They were all mine to discover and explore and make my own. You wouldn't believe how good that made me feel.

I walked to the end of the fencing and carried on along the road. If I cut round by the copse, skirting the edge of it, I should be able to double back and make it round to the back of the hotel where the grounds were. Me and my mates had fixed the short wire fencing round the back so that we could get in and out without anyone realizing. All we had to do was push the wire mesh back into place when we'd finished.

Once my mate Dave was stupid enough to try and get through without pushing the mesh all the way up and the wire sliced through his leg like a sharp knife through a squishy tomato. You should've seen the blood pour. I tied my belt around his leg to try and stem the bleeding and then we had to practically carry him all the way back to the main road. Stopping at the first house we came to, we finally managed to call for an ambulance. They rushed him to hospital but fast. He needed twelve stitches and a blood transfusion. My mates weren't too keen on the place after that. But something kept drawing me back. It was a great place that deserved a good owner. Someone who would take care of it as it should be taken care of.

But the tunnels were mine.

At least for a little while.

At least for tonight.

11. Andrew

'Yeah, that's right! The wrinklies are next door. Hang on a sec!' Andrew flopped down on the bed, swinging his legs around so that he lay prone. He moved his mobile phone to his other ear, away from the wall, announcing, 'In this dive, the walls are probably as thin as tissue paper.'

'Your mum still flapping over you?' asked Kieran at the other end of the phone.

'What d'you think? Still, at least I've got my own room – not that it's up to much.'

'What's the hotel like?' asked Kieran.

'Have a guess! If we weren't leaving on Sunday, I'd be tearing my hair out. Goodness knows why Mum thought it would be such a great birthday treat for me. But guess what? There's a girl here—'

'That didn't take you long!' Kieran laughed.

'You know me! Anyway, her name is Rainbow but she calls herself Raye.'

'Rainbow? Love and peace, man!' laughed Kieran. 'So what's she like?'

'She's OK, actually.'

'Ooh!'

'I mean, she's a bit of a whippet but in a land of dogs, she's the least canine . . .' Andrew amended hastily.

'A whippet?'

'Yeah, you know – skinny. You could probably use her ribs as a toast rack. But she'll do.'

'High praise indeed!'

'I'm not joking. From what I've seen so far, the girls

down here should walk around with paper bags on their heads and do us all a favour . . .'

Kieran's burst of laughter over the mobile phone could be heard from across the room. 'So, are you going to make a move on her?'

'Of course. I've got nothing else to do.'

'I bet her parents watch her like a hawk.'

'So? She fancies me something rotten so that's half my work done for me already!'

'I bet you don't even get the chance to pucker up!' Kieran scoffed.

'Wanna bet?'

'You're on! I bet you don't get to snog her before you leave on Sunday.'

'Oh, please! Don't insult me. Can't you come up with something a bit more challenging than that?' Andrew said disdainfully.

'Talk is cheap.'

'What kind of cheap are we talking about?' Andrew challenged.

'What did you have in mind?' Kieran asked.

Andrew laughed before mentioning a sum of money.

'The last of the big spenders!' Kieran was not impressed.

'That's all any of the girls down here are worth,' said Andrew.

'Right then. You're on! But you've got to provide proof that she kissed you.'

'How do I do that?'

'That's your problem,' said Kieran.

'OK,' Andrew replied. 'I almost feel guilty about taking your money off you. Almost . . . but not quite! The girl's practically eating out of my hand already. You should've seen the way she looked at me. She obviously has first-class taste and knows a good thing when she sees it!'

'You don't think much of yourself, do you?' said Kieran.

'If I don't love myself, who else will!'

'Hmm! So how d'you plan to do this?'

'I'm going to find Rainbow and chat to her. Let her see my sensitive side.' Andrew grinned.

'Good luck, but don't forget, it doesn't count unless you can prove it.'

'Don't worry. I and my proof will be with you on Monday!'

Andrew hung up, throwing his phone down on the bed. Placing his hands behind his head, he smirked up at the ceiling. And in the corner of the room, unseen by Andrew, stood Liam, listening to every word.

12. Acquaintances

'Miss Dawn, will you be leaving any time soon?'

'Miss Eve, I might ask you the same question.'

The two elderly women sat regarding each other, smiles serene, eyes like diamonds, minds like steel traps. They were closer than sisters, but they weren't friends. They called themselves 'acquaintances'. To everyone else they were travelling companions and rarely apart. The two women were currently sharing adjacent rooms at the Phoenix Manor Hotel.

'So who have you got your eye on now?' asked Miss Eve.

Miss Dawn scrutinized Miss Eve before answering, 'Mr Jackman – as if you didn't know. I saw you talking to Nova earlier. What were you doing? Asking about me – or Mr Jackman?'

'What makes you think you have anything to do with it?' Miss Eve huffed. 'The world doesn't revolve around you, you know.'

Miss Dawn smiled serenely. Miss Eve glowered at her.

'So you're after Mr Jackman, eh?' asked Miss Eve, trying to show that she wasn't rankled. 'Now, he's definitely edible!'

'Put him down! Besides, he's mine!'

'I do like to see a woman of your advanced years still living in hope,' taunted Miss Eve.

'Hope is my middle name,' Miss Dawn said silkily. 'You should know that by now.'

Miss Eve considered her companion. 'So you reckon you'll get him?'

'I know I will.' Miss Dawn's smile had returned.

'That's what you said about the last three, and it didn't happen, did it? I got them.'

'It'll be different this time. I can feel it in my vitals.'

'That's what you said the last three times.'

'I have faith,' said Miss Dawn.

'Faith?' scoffed Miss Eve.

'Yes, faith.'

'An extinct commodity.'

'Dormant perhaps, not extinct.'

'On the way out,' argued Miss Eve.

'Or on the way in. It all depends on your point of view.'

Miss Eve tried and failed to keep the irritation out of her voice. 'Why d'you always have to argue?'

'Why do you?'

'You really are the most aggravating creature,'

'I know!' Miss Dawn's serene smile broadened.

'I could always move on, you know.'

'Not without me you couldn't,' said Miss Dawn. 'Where one of us goes, the other follows – remember?'

Miss Eve glared at her companion, then suddenly smiled. 'I don't know why I'm worried. Mr Jackman *is* going to disappoint you.'

'Why?'

'Why what?'

'Why're you so sure he will?'

'You expect too much. You always do.'

'He'll do the right thing,' said Miss Dawn. But was that the faintest trace of doubt in her voice?

'Ah, but his idea of the "right thing" might not be the same as yours,' Miss Eve said with glee.

'We'll see,' said Miss Dawn. 'We'll see.'

13. Liam and Rainbow

'Hello, Rainbow.'

Raye whirled round, ready to do battle with whoever it was using her full name. Only her words of rebuke withered and died on her lips. Omigod! Another gorgeous guy, with short black hair and the most beautiful brown eyes she'd ever seen. Attractive guys to the left. Handsome guys to the right. This was much more like it!

'It's Raye. I prefer Raye.'

'Of course. I prefer Raye too. Rainbow is a bit "hippy chick", isn't it!'

'Excuse me?'

'Not that I don't like Rainbow too. I do,' the boy amended hastily. 'It's just . . . it's just time for me to shut up now!'

'Can I help you with something?' Raye asked, her tone decidedly cool now.

'You can help me take my foot out of my mouth!'

Raye smiled reluctantly. 'So you're a guest here? Did you arrive this morning?'

'No. I've been here a while. I live . . . round here.'

'Really? I haven't seen you before,' said Rainbow.

'Nova has. I like to walk around the grounds. I love it up here. I hope that's OK?'

Raye shrugged. 'It's fine with me. So how come you know my name?'

'I made it my business to find out. I'm Liam.'

Raye held out her hand. 'Hi, Liam.'

Liam put his hands behind his back. Raye's hand dropped to her side. What was this guy's problem?

'I'm sorry. My hands are dirty,' said Liam quickly, his hands now lightly clenched at his sides.

Raye glanced down. Hmm! His hands didn't look particularly dirty to her. 'Why did you make it your business to find out my name?' she asked.

'I just did. Look, there was something else I wanted to talk to you about.'

'I'm list —' Raye's head snapped back with sudden shock. For the briefest of moments she could've sworn she could actually see *through* Liam. She shook her head and blinked heavily. The light in the reception hall was playing funny tricks with her eyes.

'I don't have much time,' Liam said in an enigmatic rush. 'Just watch out for Andrew, OK? He's a liar.'

'I beg your pardon?'

'He wants to use you to win a stupid bet.'

'How d'you know that?'

'I just know, that's all.'

Raye regarded Liam. 'You're just trying to stir things, aren't you? What's your game?'

'I'm not the one playing games, Andrew is. Look, I have to go now,' Liam said apologetically. 'But I'm not lying.'

'And I'm not listening. The nerve of some people!' Raye turned and stormed off towards the dining room.

She turned to laser Liam with one last glare, but he'd vanished. Raye looked around, annoyed. He must've gone down the same rat hole he came out of. How come he knew Andrew? And why was he trying to make trouble between them? And if he lived round there, how come she'd never seen him before? Raye thought she'd thoroughly scouted out all the local talent — not that there was that much! So she would've definitely noticed someone like Liam.

Next time she saw him, he wouldn't get off so lightly. She'd have a few choice words of her own to say and Liam wasn't going anywhere until he'd heard every single one.

14. Nova

Nova sat on her favourite bench beneath a pergola at the far end of the hotel grounds. The pergola separated the bench from the direct gaze of the hotel and all around were the scents and sights of autumn – damask roses and late honeysuckle. Not that Nova was there to admire the flowers. Her head turned first one way, then the other, the expression on her face alert and watchful.

'Liam? Are you here?' Nova whispered. 'I'm sorry – OK?'

Nothing. Nova had been right through the hotel, calling out to Liam and looking for him. She'd even tried the guest rooms – at least, the ones that weren't locked or occupied. For all she knew, Liam could've been sitting right next to her at that moment. Nova reached out a tentative hand, only to drop it back down by her side. No, he wasn't there. Even as he had faded out in her room, she could still sense him. She'd known the moment he was no longer present and that had been several seconds after his voice had faded. He wasn't here. As far as Nova could tell, he wasn't anywhere. Nova heard footsteps turning the corner, crunching on the gravel path. She sprang to her feet.

Liam . . .?

'Oh, sorry. I didn't know anyone was here.' Mr Jackman was already turning round.

'It's OK,' Nova said quickly. 'I was just leaving.'

'You don't have to leave on my account.'

'I'm not. I really was going. I just like to sit here sometimes. It's peaceful.'

'I like it here too.' Mr Jackman nodded, looking around. 'And you can smell the sea, even if you can't see it from this spot!'

Nova was surprised at the sudden volunteering of information. She knew she should probably leave him to it, but for some reason her feet didn't seem to want to move.

'Don't you think the sea smells like a promise?' Mr Jackman mused. 'A promise of all the things it knows and all the things it might reveal.'

Nova frowned at him. What on earth was he going on about? Did he get all poetic with everyone who stayed around long enough? Maybe that was why most of the guests gave him a wide berth. Except Miss Dawn, who had taken him under her wing.

In a flash it came back to her. Nova now remembered the rest of what Miss Dawn had said to her that morning. It had been about Mr Jackman. And was that what Miss Eve had been trying to get out of her when they went for their walk which was mercifully cut short? Nova wondered at the elderly women's interest in Mr Jackman.

'I love this place,' said Mr Jackman on a sigh. 'Always have.'

'You've been here before?' said Nova.

A trace of a smile flitted over Mr Jackman's face. 'A while ago.'

'I can't remember seeing you before.' Not that Nova remembered every hotel guest who'd ever stayed at the hotel, but somehow she knew she would've remembered Mr Jackman.

'It was some time ago . . . Are your family happy here? Your sister?'

'Why d'you ask?'

'Just something I heard her say a couple of days ago,' said Mr Jackman. 'It sounded as if she wasn't too keen on the place.'

'Don't listen to Raye. She's never happy unless she's whingeing about something.'

'Your mum and dad are OK here though, aren't they?'

'They are now. They weren't at first – well, Mum wasn't,' Nova amended.

'Why did your mum and dad move down here then?' asked Mr Jackman.

'The hotel was left to my mum by a great-aunt,' Nova explained. 'It was called the Manor Hotel then. Mum and Dad decided to put all their savings into doing it up and opening it as a hotel again.'

'Yes, I remember the Manor Hotel,' said Mr Jackman thoughtfully.

'Is that when you stayed here last?'

'No. I used to live round here,' said Mr Jackman. 'I much prefer its new name – Phoenix Manor Hotel.'

'Mum and Dad decided to call it that.'

'It suits the place. Your name is Nova, isn't it?'

Nova nodded, surprised.

'And your mum's name is Karmah?'

'That's right. Dad wanted me and Raye to have names like Mum.'

'And what did your mum think of that?'

Nova laughed. 'Apparently they agreed that Mum should name any boys they had and Dad would name the girls. And a deal's a deal.'

'I see!' Mr Jackman smiled.

Nova smiled back. 'So where d'you live now?'

Mr Jackman turned to look at her. Really look at her.

'That was nosy,' Nova said quickly.

'No, you're all right . . . I have a flat in Manchester. I wouldn't say I live there, though. I travel around too much.'

'With your job?'

'Something like that,' said Mr Jackman. 'I like to keep moving – even when I don't have to.'

'Why?'

'I'm searching.'

'For what?'

'Someone.'

'Who?'

Mr Jackman looked at Nova and grinned.

Nova's face started to burn. 'Sorry! That was nosy too.'

'Yes, it was. But good for you!'

Nova studied Mr Jackman, not making any attempt to disguise what she was doing. Strange, but when he grinned, someone else's face had flashed through her mind quicker than summer lightning. Nova tried to remember just who it was Mr Jackman reminded her of, but it was gone.

'So who are you looking for?' she repeated.

She waited for him to answer her last question – but he didn't. As Nova watched his smile fade, she realized it was the first time she'd seen him smile since he'd arrived at the hotel. He didn't look like a man who smiled easily.

'I like your name,' Mr Jackman said at last. 'It suits you. Super Nova!'

Nova smiled wanly. If he was aiming for a subtle change of subject, he'd failed miserably.

'Sorry! I bet that's not the first time you've had someone say that to you,' said Mr Jackman.

'No.'

It was only about the fifty millionth time she'd heard

the same joke! They stood in silence for a few strangely unawkward moments. Nova continued to scrutinize Mr Jackman. She usually knew what to make of the guests within five minutes of spotting them. The arrogant, the shy, the considerate, those with something to hide, the pompous – it didn't take her long to suss them out. But Mr Jackman was different. Strange that he should now decide to talk to her – especially after Nova's earlier conversation with Miss Dawn. This was the most he'd said to anyone in the hotel since he'd arrived, as far as she knew.

'Are you here for a holiday or are you still searching?' she asked.

'Still searching,' replied Mr Jackman. 'I never stop. I never will.'

Nova waited and wondered if Mr Jackman was going to continue. It wasn't like having a conversation with anyone else she had ever met. Usually you could tell by what was said, and how it was said and the way the person looked, just where the conversation was going and whether or not it had finished. But not with Mr Jackman. With him it was all guesswork.

'I'd better be getting back,' she sighed.

Mr Jackman nodded, moving past her to sit on the bench she had just vacated. Nova glanced back at him. What was it Miss Dawn had said? 'We all need friends'? She wondered why Mr Jackman had suddenly decided to speak to her. Maybe Miss Dawn was right. But it wouldn't have surprised or upset her to learn that Mr Jackman had forgotten about her already. He had himself and his quest and he didn't seem to need anything else.

Nova headed back to the hotel. Why worry about Mr Jackman? He was old enough to take care of himself. He certainly didn't need her help for anything. But as Nova took one last look at him, it occurred to her that she'd never seen anyone look so lonely. Or quite so alone.

15. Mr Jackman

'I need your help . . .' Mr Jackman stared straight ahead but his thoughts were light years away in long ago. 'D'you hear me? I need your help. It's in your hands now. I've been everywhere. This is the only place left. And I'm not leaving. Not until I find you. You shouldn't have gone. It wasn't your fault, I know that. It was my fault. I drove you out. That's why I'm not leaving. But you have to help me.

'You have to.

'You just have to . . .'

16. Nova and Rainbow

'Rainbow, stop picking at your food and eat it properly.'

'My name is Raye,' Rainbow amended tersely. 'And I *am* eating.'

Mum frowned down at Rainbow's dinner plate. 'Eating what exactly? Air?'

'Food!' said Rainbow. 'And I'm fifteen, Mum, not five. I don't need you to tell me to eat my food. You'll be picking up the fork and feeding me next.'

'Raye, ten minutes ago you had a dollop of mashed potato on your plate, along with two sausages and baked beans – and none of them have moved,' said Mum.

'I've eaten some beans,' argued Raye.

'No, you haven't.'

Raye glared at Mum. Her voice dropped an octave as she mockingly said, '"I put it to you, Rainbow Clibbens, that you had one hundred and fifty beans on your plate at the start of the meal and there are still one hundred and fifty left." What did you do, Mum? Count them onto my plate so you could count them all off again?'

Nova slowly chewed on her sausage as she listened to her mum and sister argue. It was the same almost every meal time.

'Raye, I didn't stand in this hot kitchen all afternoon making you dinner for the fun of it.'

'Here we go.' Raye tutted and raised her eyes heavenwards. '"I spend all day in this kitchen, and do you appreciate it? Hell, no!"'

'Don't be so cheeky.'

'Stop bossing me about then.'

'I'll stop when you start eating. Or should I get your dad to have a word with you?'

Raye savagely pronged a sausage before stuffing the whole thing into her mouth in one go. 'Satisfied?' she mumbled, her cheeks bulging.

Nova and the twins exchanged a long-suffering look. Nova shook her head as she took another bite of her sausage.

'Can't you two stop arguing for two seconds?' Jake asked.

'Yeah! You're giving us a bellyache,' Jude added.

'And you're both giving me a headache,' Nova put in her twopence worth, glaring at her mum, then at Raye in turn.

'Fine! Right!' Raye piled creamy-white mashed potato onto her fork so that the fork was no longer visible beneath the huge mound. Then she pushed the whole lot into her mouth.

'Good idea, Raye,' Mum said sarcastically. 'Choking on your food will really show me!'

Raye sat in stony silence and continued chewing her food. Her eyes shot daggers at anyone who dared to look in her direction. Nova cut carefully into her second sausage, dissecting it into four equal pieces, before pushing one of the quarters into her mouth. She had a set routine. Peas, beans or tomatoes first, then the meat – whatever it might be, then the energy food (as Mum called it), or stodge (as Raye called it). Stodge like chips or rice or mashed potatoes or pasta. Nova never argued about eating her food. And she always finished what she was given. She looked down at her plate. Nearly there. She popped another quarter of sausage into her mouth.

'Mum, can I have some more milk?' asked Jake.

'Me too!' added Jude.

Mum turned round to get the milk out of the fridge. Nova spread some mashed potato over her last two pieces of sausage. She popped one into her mouth before pushing the remaining mashed potato into a miniature volcano-shaped heap in the middle of the plate.

'Mum, while you're in the fridge, can I have something fizzy to drink?' asked Nova.

'Like what?'

'Got any ginger beer?'

'There's one left,' Mum replied.

'I'll have that then. Thanks.' Nova put the last lot of mashed potato and sausage into her mouth before putting her knife and fork together in the middle of her plate.

'I see you've finished all your food – again. Creep!' Raye hissed.

'What's your problem?' asked Nova. 'Not enough fibre in your diet?'

'Crawly creeper!' Raye mustered as much venom as she could to inject into her words.

'I think you mean creepy crawler! You're such a pleasure to be around – really,' said Nova. 'I'm so proud you're my sister.'

'Bog off!'

'You first,' said Nova.

'That's quite enough of that,' Mum snapped.

Nova and Raye glared at each other. Jude and Jake shared a grin. Meal times were such fun, with everyone arguing and saying rude things.

'I'll help you to serve the dinner later, Mum,' said Raye, reluctant to tear the full force of her filthy look away from her sister.

'Catch me, someone,' said Mum, swooning. 'I'm fainting!'

'You're always going on about me helping around the

hotel more and when I do volunteer, you just mock me,' Raye fumed.

'You need a sense of humour transplant,' Nova muttered so she could be heard.

'And who was talking to you?' said Raye.

'Sorry, Raye.' Mum straightened up. 'You're quite right. I shouldn't have made fun of you. Thanks for volunteering.'

'She just wants to be with whatshisface – Andrew,' said Jake.

'Are you going to snog him?' asked Jude in all seriousness.

After one last razor-sharp look which scythed around the table, Raye flounced out of the room. Mum shook her head and handed a can of ginger beer over to Nova.

'I can't wait to be a teenager.' Jude grinned at his brother.

'Me too!' agreed Jake.

'Just drink your milk, you two!' said Mum, placing a full glass before each of the twins.

Nova drank as much of her ginger beer in one go as she could, until her stomach was full to the point of being bloated. She sat back and stared at her empty plate. Totally empty. Only a little tomato sauce from the beans showed there'd been anything on it. Nova rubbed her stomach. The gas from the ginger beer was making her feel really uncomfortable. It couldn't be a good idea to gulp it down so fast. The effect was always the same. Nova sighed and stood up. Standing across the table from her was Liam.

She jumped. 'How long have you been standing there?' she asked.

'We're not standing. We're still sitting,' Jude frowned.

'She's not talking to us,' Jake whispered in Jude's ear.

'I was talking to . . . Never mind.' No way was Nova

going to try and explain herself again. She turned back to Liam. 'How long have you been here?'

'Long enough,' Liam replied. 'I need your help.'

'To do what?'

'You've got to help me get my — get Mr Jackman out of here.'

'Out of the hotel?' asked Nova.

'Yes.'

'Why? What's he done?'

'Nova, who're you talking to?' Mum asked.

'No one. Myself.' Nova headed for the kitchen door. She'd have to watch it. If she started talking to Liam when her family were around, they'd all think she was barking mad. Well . . . even more barking mad than usual.

'Er, oh no you don't,' Mum called Nova back. 'It's your turn to help me load up the dishwasher.'

'But, Mum, I've got other things to do.'

'Tough!' said Mum, without a single shred of sympathy. 'It's your turn. Get on with it.'

'But, Mum . . .'

'Nova . . .'

Nova turned back to Liam with a regretful shrug, but he was gone.

17. Liam and Mr Jackman

'When're you going to leave?'

Mr Jackman sat at the small wooden table, its surface scratched and scarred, and continued to write. He didn't even raise his head.

'I want you to leave . . .'

Mr Jackman raised his head, a frown creeping across his face, but all too soon he carried on with his writing.

'D'you hear me? You're not wanted here. Why don't you go?' Liam shouted from the middle of the room. 'You made my life a misery when I was alive and now I'm dead, you're still doing it!'

Liam glared at the man before him in total frustration. He tried to force himself to focus so that he could materialize, but all the old feelings kept bubbling up inside him. It was so hard, deliberately appearing in front of people. It always seemed to happen by accident, when he lost his temper or experienced some other emotion equally potent. Except with Nova. Why did she see him so easily when no one else could? And now, unless he faded out and thought himself somewhere else entirely, Nova could see him whether he wanted her to or not. Liam sighed. What was the reason? There had to be a reason. Maybe she was more sensitive to his presence? Or maybe she just wanted to see him more than anyone else in the hotel. *Needed* to see him. Needed his help – just as he needed her help at this moment. Tentatively, he moved closer. What was this man doing? What was it that had him so engrossed?

Liam walked over to stand to one side of the man and

began to read over his shoulder. Horrified, he shook his head, unable to believe what he was reading – but it was there in black and white. He looked at the man beside him, hoping against hope that he'd misread the letter. Maybe he'd misunderstood what was written? But the sombre expression on the man's face told Liam that he'd done no such thing.

'Oh God!' Liam exclaimed.

He needed to find help – fast. And there wasn't much time.

18. Liam

I moved swiftly through the hotel grounds, looking around all the time to make sure there was no one else there. Luckily the slab that marked out the entrance to the tunnel didn't have too much debris over it. Just an old, discarded wheelbarrow, recently dumped. Shifting it to one side, I moved the slab covering the entrance. I sat down at the edge of the now uncovered hole, then twisted my body round to grab hold of the rope ladder which led down to the tunnels below. Moving down a couple of rungs, I leaned against the ladder and the dirt wall beyond that, until I was steady enough to pull the slab back into place. Even partially hollowed out, it was heavy, but nothing I couldn't handle.

I was careful to make sure the slab was back in place before I headed down the ladder. I didn't want anyone to find the entrance. I was the one who'd gone to the trouble of replacing the rotten, knotted rope which used to hang at the entrance. I'd made the ladder I was now standing on, buying several metres of rope and twisting and plaiting them into shape in my every spare moment until it was ready. So why should I give up this place?

The tunnels were warm and dry, just as I remembered them. But I'd barely taken three steps before my thoughts returned once again to Josh. I'd told him all about the tunnels, but until now I'd refused to show them to him. But why not? If I was going to show them to anyone in the world it would be him. After all, he is my brother and I care about him. Who am I trying to kid? I love him. There! I admit it! And strangely enough, I don't feel silly or soppy or even embarrassed. In fact, for some strange reason, it makes me feel . . . OK! Not just OK about my brother, but in a strange way, OK about myself as well.

So what was Josh doing now? Wondering where I was? What

was I worried about? The fact that Josh might be anxious about me, or the fact that he might not be? I smiled wryly as I thought about my younger brother. He had a lot to answer for! I shone my torch around. The dim, yellow torchlight was soon swallowed whole by the darkness. Ahead, behind, it made no difference. I could see no further than a metre in any direction. The torch was a whip, cracking silently to keep the gloom and shadows at bay. But I'd only been walking for about ten or fifteen minutes when it began to flicker. I turned the torch upwards to stare into its fading light. How could the batteries be dying? I'd changed them less than a fortnight ago. I shone it on the ground, looking for a patch of ground that was even. About a metre ahead of me was the perfect bed — ground that was even and solid. I lay down, taking off my jacket so I could use it as a pillow. Switching off the torch to save the batteries, I made myself comfortable and within moments I surprised myself by falling fast asleep.

I woke with a start and with that groggy feeling you get from too much sleep rather than not enough. I could hear a faint rumbling sound but I couldn't tell which direction it was coming from. It must've been the noise that woke me up, faint as it was. Usually the tunnels were eerily silent. I stood up, wiping the sleep out of my eyes. The tunnels were still pitch black but I instinctively knew it was now morning. I glanced down at my watch, forgetting I couldn't see a thing. I felt around for my torch, then shone the light down on it. Ten-thirty. I'd been asleep for ages. I must've been more tired than I thought. That probably explained why I'd been so ratty to my brother. Never mind. I'd make it up to him. I always did.

And maybe it was time to make up with Dad too?

To be honest, I was tired of fighting with him. Time to call a truce — if Dad would meet me halfway. He had to be just as sick of our quarrels as I was. When I was a lot younger, we'd go to the beach or the local museum, or play football, or just sit huddled up on the sofa watching the telly. Yes, he was my dad, but it was more than that. We were good mates. Until Mum died. He fell to pieces and our family fell apart. And stupidly I'd thought I could put everyone and everything back together. Sitting there in the torch-lit gloom, I saw more clearly than I ever had before. When Mum died, and Dad fell apart, I'd tried to take over his role. But I couldn't. I shouldn't have even tried. I needed help – Dad's help. I took a deep breath and let it out slowly, one fight, one quarrel, one bad thought, one frustration at a time. Time to let go. Time to go home. Time to start again.

I gathered up my jacket, switched on my torch and turned, heading back for the tunnel entrance. The torchlight was dim, but it'd last until I was out of the tunnels. After a couple of minutes I stopped abruptly. What was that noise? I stopped breathing, moving my head forward to listen into the silence. A faint cracking sound . . . What was it? And a rumble, like some kind of machinery, or thunder. What was going on?

Get a grip, I told myself. My imagination was starting to play tricks on me. Funny that! Mr Sugarman, my English teacher, was always whining at me for not having enough imagination.

'Liam, switch on your imagination when you write!'

'Liam, this poem lacks imagination. Don't you daydream? Can't you think above and beyond and outside your little box?'

Outside my little box! Patronizing twit! What did that mean, for heaven's sake? I had enough problems coping with my dad and Josh and everyday stuff without drifting along with my head in the clouds.

Without warning the torch went out and I was plunged into darkness. I shook the torch vigorously. Nothing. It was so dark, I couldn't even see the torch in my hand, let alone anything else. I looked around, careful not to move my feet, only my head. The darkness was an impenetrable, overpowering force, swallowing me up, eyes first. A darkness rich and thick enough to drink. I took a cautious step forward. I'd be OK as long as I didn't panic. I'd been in these tunnels a dozen times or more – so what was there to panic about? One foot in front of the other. Face forward. Keep going. No problem. I took another step – and another. See! This was easy. No string, no twine, no thread, no nothing. I didn't need it. Usually I only used twine if I was exploring a new part of the tunnels, but when I stormed out of the house, I didn't even know where I was going until I found myself at the hotel. I'd been in the tunnels before and I could find my way through the familiar bits with my eyes shut.

So as long as I didn't get lost . . . but I wouldn't. And if I did, I'd just call out until someone heard me, so I wasn't in danger. OK, I shouldn't have been in the tunnels in the first place but I could argue about that afterwards. The quarrel I'd had with Dad last night had been a scorcher – by both our standards. But if I could want to go home and face Dad, then I could face anything.

I started walking again, my hands out in front of me. I had to be only seconds away from the exit. I'd feel the rope ladder and be out before I could string five thoughts together. No problem. I shook my torch and tried switching it on and off again. Nothing. Then I dropped it.

'Hell!' The word exploded into the darkness around me.

I squatted down to fumble around in the dirt for my torch. I swept my hand across the dirt in ever-increasing arcs. My hand swept over something small and furry – and moving. Instantly, I drew back my hand, wiping it on my jeans. I couldn't help the shudder that ricocheted through me. I didn't even want to know what that was. My feet swivelled on the dry earth as I felt around again. Stupid Josh must've been playing with my torch and drained the batteries. My lips thinned into a angry frown. 'Just wait till I get hold of you, Josh,' I muttered.

At last I found the torch. I had to really stretch out to get it. It must've rolled away from me. But as I straightened up, I realized instinctively that I wasn't facing in exactly the same direction. My feet had moved slightly to the right. So all I had to do was move them a quarter turn to the left. Too much or too little? I couldn't be that off track. Just keep going. Whatever happens, just keep going.

I wanted to go home. I wasn't afraid, but these tunnels were like a maze, with tunnels off more tunnels, and I didn't want to get lost in the darkness. I carried on walking. I was OK. Just walk in a straight line back to the tunnel entrance. See! Easy!

Crack!

I stopped in my tracks and looked straight up. What was that?

Cra-a-ck! What felt like dry rain fell over my face. I leapt back and wiped the dirt and dust from out of my eyes. There was that sound again. And then panic grabbed me. And all I wanted to do was run. Move. Get out of there — as fast as I could. I started running. But before I could take more than three strides, the cracking sound turned into a deafening roar and the rain of dust and dirt was just the start of something far worse. I hit the ground, trying to protect my head with my arms as the world fell on top of me and all I knew was darkness and the sound of thunder. And then the world changed from pitch black to a cold, ice white which blinded me and froze every part of my body until I shattered into a million pieces.

19. Liam

Liam stood outside the toilet cubicle listening to the sounds of someone inside being violently sick. He shook his head, his frown cutting into his cheeks as he listened. It was like clockwork. Within half an hour of every meal time, she'd be in here, making herself vomit. He could set his watch by her – if it'd been working instead of permanently stuck at 10.37.

What was the matter with her family? Couldn't her mum and dad see what was going on? Didn't they notice the pattern to her eating? Insisting on certain foods with every meal and always eating them first. Always guzzling orange juice or fizzy drinks after eating. Disappearing after every meal and then reappearing a little while later to look listless and sombre. Being tired all the time. The signs were all there. And then there was the bingeing on snack foods. She'd sneak up to her room with two or three packets of crisps or a packet of custard creams or fruit shortcake biscuits, followed half an hour later by the famous disappearing act into her favourite toilet cubicle. Liam was sure that if he were her dad or one of her brothers, he'd have been very suspicious about her behaviour. OK, so her mum and dad were busy running the hotel, but that was a reason, not an excuse.

Liam shook his head again. The toilet was flushed and the sound was followed by a racking cough. Then came the sound of more retching. Liam turned away in disgust. He couldn't stay there all day listening to her cough her guts out – he had things to do. There had to be some way to solve his problem without involving her. But how? Liam faded out slowly, shaking his head.

Time was running out.

20. Dinner

'Can I get you anything else, Andrew?' asked Raye.

'No thanks,' Andrew smiled. 'And please say thanks to your mum and dad for such a delicious meal.'

'Yes, it was,' Mr Stanley chorused.

'It was lovely,' Mrs Stanley agreed after a pointed look from her husband.

'I'll tell Mum. It'll make a change, someone actually enjoying her cooking!' said Raye.

Andrew's smile was warm as Raye gathered up his plate. She stood beside him, returning his smile with interest as they regarded each other.

'Raye, I think we've finished as well,' said Mr Stanley gently.

Raye forced her eyes away. 'Yes, of course.' Reluctantly she moved away from Andrew and continued round the table.

'Any chance of us getting our dessert before I'm too old to have the teeth left to chew it?' Miss Eve called from an adjacent table.

'There's no hurry.' Miss Dawn smiled sympathetically at Raye.

'I'll be right there,' Raye promised. Very professionally, she gathered up the rest of the plates on Andrew's table and turned to head for the door.

'Remind me to come back as a boy next time,' Miss Eve grumbled. 'Then I might actually get some pudding from that girl this side of Christmas.'

Raye turned to glare at her, before she carried on out of the dining room. Andrew leapt up and ran across to her.

'Let me get that door for you,' he said.

'Thanks.' Raye's smile was dazzling.

Andrew held open the dining-room door, despite the fact that it swung open with the lightest push.

'Thanks again,' said Raye, wishing she could think of something more scintillating to say.

'Would you like to go for a walk with me some time tomorrow?' asked Andrew.

'Where?'

'Maybe down to the beach?'

'That'd be lovely,' Raye enthused. Her face fell. 'But I've got to help around the hotel in the afternoon and then I've got to finish my homework so I can probably only get away straight after breakfast.'

'That's fine with me,' Andrew nodded. 'I'll meet you just outside the hotel?'

'It's a date.' Raye's smile shone out.

'It's a date,' Andrew agreed and headed back to his mum and dad's table.

Raye did her best not to grin from ear to ear. If Mum saw she'd instantly start asking questions. Raye bustled into the kitchen, her tray stacked with dirty dinner plates, most of which were surprisingly empty. Nova was at the table, preparing more desserts while Mum refilled the coffee machine with fresh coffee grounds.

'Your pie is going down well,' Raye told Mum.

'It is, isn't it?' Mum looked dubiously at the two slices of pie she had left in the baking tray. More often than not, she made two trays-worth of food and at least one tray was still left over at the end of the evening. She'd have to try that tinned lamb as a pie filling again.

'Miss Eve wants her dessert,' said Raye.

'Over there on the counter.' Mum pointed.

Raye picked up a clean tray and placed two bowls of

peach and raspberry strudel on it – one with custard from a tin, one with soft scoop vanilla ice cream.

'Nova, can you manage that coffee for Mr Jackman?' asked Raye.

'No problem.'

'He's in the alcove,' Raye told her.

'Why d'you put him in there?' Mum turned to Raye.

'I didn't seat him. Nova did,' Raye defended herself.

'Before you have a go at me, he asked for it specifically,' said Nova. 'Said he wanted some privacy.'

'There's a surprise,' Raye muttered.

Nova shook her head. 'I wonder what's wrong with the poor man. I feel sorry for him.'

'Why?' Raye was scornful. 'It's his choice not to make friends with anyone.'

'Maybe it's not that simple —' Nova began.

'Oh, Nova, don't start!' Raye begged. 'You're always trying to create mysteries around people. He's just an anti-social loner, so let's leave him alone.'

'I was only saying,' Nova huffed. 'No need to jump down my throat.'

Raising her eyebrows in exasperation, Raye gathered up a number of dessert menus and headed out of the kitchen, followed by her sister. They both entered the dining room and split like a fork in the road to hand out their various items. Nova concentrated on the coffee on her small tray, determined not to spill a drop. A quick glance up to make sure she wasn't about to trip over anyone's leg or bag, and she made her way to Mr Jackman's table. The dining room was L-shaped, with a secluded booth at the end of the alcove that formed the shorter section of the room. Mum liked everyone to mix and mingle and never seated anyone in the alcove unless nothing else was available. But Mr Jackman always asked for the alcove table when he ate in the dining room with the other guests, which wasn't often. Nova kept her head down, her eyes still focused on her coffee. She turned the corner and made her way down to the last table. It was only when she'd dodged past the only other unoccupied table in the alcove that she glanced up again – and stopped dead in her tracks.

Liam was sitting opposite Mr Jackman at his table.

'Liam, what . . .?' Nova's lips snapped together. She had to remember not to talk to him in front of other people.

Mr Jackman stared at her. 'What did you say?'

'Nothing.'

Mr Jackman sprang to his feet. 'What did you say?' he urged.

Nova stared at him. She glanced at Liam, who vigorously shook his head. 'I just said . . . erm . . . what . . . what did you order to drink? I just wanted to check I've brought this coffee to the right table.'

Mr Jackman slowly sat down again. 'Oh, I see.'

Nova was glad he did, because she didn't. 'Is something wrong, Mr Jackman?'

'I thought you said . . . something else.'

'What?'

Mr Jackman shook his head. 'It doesn't matter. The coffee is mine.'

'There you are.' Nova put the cup and saucer down on the table, adding a small jug of milk and a tiny bowl of brown and white sugar cubes. It was so hard to carry on as if there was nothing unusual happening with Liam sitting there watching her every move.

'Nova, I need your help. You can't let him leave the hotel tonight. You must find a way to stop him,' Liam urged.

'What?' Nova wasn't sure if she'd heard correctly.

'I didn't say anything,' said Mr Jackman.

'D'you understand me, Nova? He plans to leave the hotel as soon as he's finished his coffee. You mustn't let him,' Liam pleaded.

'How am I meant to do that?'

'Who're you talking to?' Mr Jackman turned his head to where Nova was looking. 'Who's there?'

'I—'

Mr Jackman grabbed Nova's arm. 'It's him, isn't it? I know it's him. I can *feel* him.'

'You're hurting me.' Nova tried to pull away.

'Tell me who you're talking to!' Mr Jackman demanded.

'Let her go!' Liam sprang up, furious.

'Liam . . .' Mr Jackman immediately let go of Nova's arm. He stared directly at Liam, his eyes huge, his mouth open and slack with stunned surprise. 'Liam . . .'

Without warning Liam swept the coffee across the table into Mr Jackman's lap.

'Ahh!' Mr Jackman yelled and sprang up like a scalded cat, pulling his hot, soaking trousers away from his skin and hopping from foot to foot.

'What on earth . . .?' Raye appeared round the corner and took in the situation at one glance. 'Nova, what on earth d'you think you're doing?' she asked furiously, rushing over. 'I'm so sorry, Mr Jackman. Nova, how could you be so clumsy?'

'I didn't do it,' Nova said indignantly.

'I suppose Mr Jackman did it to himself,' Raye fumed.

'Don't worry about it,' Mr Jackman said through gritted teeth, pulling the fabric of his trousers away from his thighs.

'We'll pay to have your trousers cleaned,' Raye said quickly.

'I didn't do it,' Nova repeated, glaring at Liam.

Liam wasn't looking at her though, or at Mr Jackman. His eyes were on Raye, with the strangest look on his face that Nova had ever seen. Liam waved a tentative hand in front of Raye's face. Raye didn't bat an eyelid. She obviously couldn't see him. His expression changed, swinging between acceptance and disappointment like a pendulum. Mr Jackman looked around, looking straight through Liam, looking past him, looking without any real focus. And Nova realized that Mr Jackman could no longer see him.

'Is he still here?' Mr Jackman asked.

Nova regarded him. How should she answer? She didn't want to answer. Mr Jackman had called Liam by his first name. How did this man know him? Who was he? And why was Liam so frightened of him? Or was it frightened for him? It was hard to tell.

'Is he here?' Mr Jackman insisted.

'Is who here?' asked Raye.

Nova looked across to where Liam was standing. Liam shook his head frantically at her.

'*Is he?*' Mr Jackman asked Nova again, ignoring her sister.

Nova nodded. 'Yes.'

'Where?'

Nova pointed.

'Prove it.'

'How?'

'Ask him who owned our house,' Mr Jackman suggested intently.

'Nova, what's he talking about?' frowned Raye.

Nova turned to Liam, but he had eyes for no one but Mr Jackman. Raye looked from Nova to Mr Jackman in turn, completely baffled. 'Would someone please tell me what's going on?' she asked.

'It was my house,' Liam said at last. 'Mum left it to me.'

'Liam says it was his. His mum left it to him,' answered Nova.

The silence that followed was only broken by the merest of sighs from Mr Jackman.

'Who's Liam?' asked Raye, irritated. 'The boy I met earlier?'

'You've met him?' Nova asked, astounded. 'So you *saw* him?'

'Of course I saw him, but he's gone now.'

'I've wanted so much to find him. I've waited so long. But I never gave up hope. I always knew I'd find him – one day.' Mr Jackman didn't look happy at the prospect though. Far from it.

'My turn now,' said Liam suddenly. 'Nova, tell him I saw the letter he was writing this afternoon. Tell him he won't succeed and all he'll do is put himself in danger if he goes through with it.'

'Through with what?' Nova asked.

'Just tell him!' Liam roared.

'Excuse me all over the place!' Nova glared, before turning back to Mr Jackman. 'Liam says he saw what you were writing earlier. He says that you won't succeed and all you'll do is put yourself in danger – so don't do it!'

Mr Jackman turned in what he thought was Liam's general direction. 'It's the only way I'll be able to find you,' he said.

Nova could tell that Mr Jackman couldn't see Liam and was just guessing at his location, but his expression was indescribable. Such hope and misery and joy and despair warring with each other for dominance on his face.

'Liam, I have to find you. I can't think of anything else.'

'Nova, tell him to go home. Tell him I don't want him here,' said Liam, adding to, and for, himself, 'He can't do anything for me. No one can.'

'Look, what am I? An answering machine?'

'Please, just tell him,' said Liam, suddenly looking dog-tired.

'Mr Jackman, he wants you to go home. He thinks you should leave here now,' Nova said, unable to keep a trace of resentment from creeping into her voice.

'Have you all gone loopy or what?' said Raye belligerently. 'Nova, if you've got together with Mr Jackman or that stupid Liam to wind me up for a joke, then I can tell you now, I'm not laughing.'

'Raye, I never—'

'Save it!' Raye turned and strode off without another word.

'I'm not leaving, Liam. Not without you,' said Mr Jackman, looking in Liam's approximate direction.

'And that, Nova, is why I didn't want him to know I was here in the first place,' Liam told her bitterly.

'Don't blame me.' Nova tried to defend herself.

'Whose fault is it then? If you weren't such a Mouth Almighty, he might've given up and gone home.'

'You're the one who just poured coffee in his lap.' Nova couldn't believe her ears.

'Liam, what happened? I need to know,' urged Mr Jackman.

Casting a look at Nova that could kill, Liam faded from view. Nova sighed. So much for trying to help.

'He . . . he's gone, hasn't he?' Mr Jackman said slowly.

'Yes,' Nova replied.

'I mean it,' Mr Jackman told her fiercely. 'I'm not

leaving this hotel without him. If he wants to get rid of me, he'll have to tell me what I want to know. Next time you see him, you tell him that.'

And with that, Mr Jackman marched past Nova and out of the dining room.

21. Liam

I got up slowly. For a terrifying moment, I had no idea where I was. No idea what the darkness around me could be. Where was I? I did have my eyes open, didn't I? I blinked a couple of times to make sure. And then I remembered.

The cave-in.

I looked around again. I still couldn't see anything. It was much too dark. But then an odd thing happened. The tunnels got strangely lighter. But not with daylight or even moonlight. This was like something I'd never seen before. It was like lying in my bed at home when it was dead dark and dead quiet, and slowly but surely being able to make out the outlines and the familiar silhouettes of the things around me. Only here, in this tunnel, I could see more clearly and more in focus than I ever could before – and it was all in the dark.

It took me a few moments to realize that.

It was as if a blue light shone out from my eyes onto all the things around me and then bounced right back at me. To be honest, it freaked me out a bit. Why could I suddenly see so clearly? There had to be blue light entering the tunnels from some place I hadn't yet been, somewhere I hadn't yet discovered. Or maybe there was some kind of luminous metallic ore in the rocks around me. Deep down, I knew I was clutching at straws but there had to be a logical explanation. I just needed to find it. Either way, I had to get out of here. Now. At once. I started walking, then running towards what I thought was the nearest exit. But I couldn't feel anything. It took a few seconds to realize that although my feet were making contact with the ground, I couldn't feel the ground against my feet, pushing back. I stopped abruptly and stared down at my feet in the cold blue semi-light.

I jumped tentatively. My feet left the ground, then seconds later they landed. I stopped. But I hadn't felt the ground that time either. The rock fall must've damaged some nerves in my legs or back. That's why I couldn't feel anything. But then, how come I could still walk and run? I didn't understand it. Terrified, I started sprinting again — in case I was running on adrenaline or luck only and one or both of them were about to run out. I should've been getting closer to the entrance by now.

But instead of getting lighter, it got darker and darker until I was racing as fast as I could, until my heart was burning and I had one hell of a stitch and still I kept running, until I was swallowed up by the dark, with nowhere left to run but onwards to nowhere.

22. Liam

Nova slammed her bedroom door shut. 'Liam, are you here?'

Liam slowly faded into view before her. 'What d'you want?'

'I want to know what all that was about?'

'All what?'

Nova's severe scowl was truly impressive. It was enough to sour milk and then some. 'Don't play games, Liam. How come Mr Jackman knows who you are?'

'That's my business,' said Liam, turning away slightly.

Nova strode towards him, aiming to grab his arm and turn him round to face her. But her hand went straight through his body. She inhaled sharply with surprise, then looked annoyed. 'I wish you wouldn't do that,' she grumbled.

'Can't help it!' Liam said with a trace of a smile.

'I mean it, Liam. What's going on between you and Mr Jackman?'

Liam's smile vanished. That was one question he wasn't going to answer. 'That's between me and him.'

'Not if you want my help, it's not.'

So that's how it was, eh? Liam scrutinized Nova carefully. 'We all have our little secrets, Nova. Even you.'

Nova suddenly grew still. 'What does that mean?'

'Never mind.'

'No, if you've got something to say, let's hear it,' Nova insisted. 'Go on.'

All right then. She'd asked for it. 'What d'you like to do in your spare time, Nova? Watch telly? Go for a walk?'

asked Liam after a pause. 'Or maybe you like to do something a little more radical? More gross but more radical?'

Nova clasped her trembling hands together in an effort to stop them from shaking.

'Shall I tell you one of my hobbies?' Liam continued. 'I love to go to the toilets on the second floor. You know, the ones at the back of the hotel? Listening to you make yourself vomit after every meal is better than watching a horror film on the telly.'

Nova's mouth fell open. 'You know?'

'Of course I know. You're in there three times a day at least, so it's either chronic long-term diarrhoea or vomiting.'

'How dare you? You have no right to spy on me!' Nova exclaimed, horrified.

'Spy on you? Do me a favour! D'you think I've got nothing better to do?'

'Obviously not!' Nova was furious. She looked like a cornered rat, looking for a fast escape route.

'Why d'you do it?' frowned Liam.

'None of your business.'

'You can dish it out but you sure can't take it, can you?' said Liam. 'How come you can ask me personal stuff, but not the other way round?'

'Because you're a ghost and ghosts don't have personal stuff,' Nova raged at him.

'Which ghost manual did you read that in?' asked Liam.

Nova clenched and unclenched her fists, desperately trying to find something to say.

'Why d'you keep making yourself sick? Is your mum's cooking really that bad?'

'It has nothing to do with Mum's cooking.'

'So what is it about then?'

'You wouldn't understand.'

'Try me.'

'It's nothing.'

'You make yourself puke morning, noon and night after every meal – but it's nothing. I believe that all right!'

'Liam, keep your nose out of my business.'

'No can do. Sorry.'

'Get out of my room.'

'No.'

'Get out of my room. Now!' Nova was fifty shades of furious.

'No!' Liam folded his arms across his chest.

'I'm not surprised you're dead!' Nova screamed at him. 'It wouldn't surprise me if someone had murdered you!'

A deathly chill flooded through Liam at Nova's words. She started to stride past him but, incensed, he grabbed her arm and yanked her back. 'Don't you ever, ever, as long as you live, say that to me again. D'you hear?' he hissed, fire dancing in his brown eyes.

Nova glared at him, but he scowled right back. She was the first to drop her gaze. 'I'm sorry. That was out of order.'

Liam's scowl didn't disappear by any means. If anything, it got worse.

'Jeez! If looks could kill . . .' Nova shot out, only to bite her lip. 'Sorry! I didn't mean that the way it came out.'

'You don't mean a lot of things, but it doesn't stop you from saying them.'

'Sorry. OK? I'm sorry. Sometimes my mouth kicks in before my brain switches on,' said Nova.

Moments ticked by as Liam struggled to control his feelings. He closed his eyes and took a concentrated deep breath. Only when he was sure he wouldn't bite her head off did he speak. 'Look, Nova, I want you to promise you'll stop all this vomiting rubbish. Apart from making your teeth rot and trashing your insides, you're too smart for all that.'

Nova pulled away from his grasp. 'What d'you know about it?'

'I know—' But Liam got no further.

'You don't know anything. People like you and my sister make me sick,' Nova interrupted harshly. 'You're all drop-dead gorgeous and you've never had to worry about more than the odd pimple. You don't know what it's like to hate every tiny bit of yourself.'

'What're you talking about?' Liam shook his head, bewildered. 'There's nothing wrong with you.'

'Yeah, right,' Nova scoffed. 'That's why when my aunts and uncles and grandparents come round, they all rave on about how beautiful Rainbow is and how sweet and cute the twins are and no one says a word about me – except maybe about how much I've shot up. "Nova, haven't you grown!", "We should call you bamboo, Nova!", "Nova, you'll soon be taller than me!"'

'What's wrong with that?'

'I hate it – OK? I hate it!' Nova shouted at him.

She ran for the door. Liam tried to grab her arm again but his hand passed right through her. He ran to get to the door first, standing in front of it to block her way. Not being able to control when he became solid was more than frustrating. Now that his initial burst of anger was over, he was back to being intangible, truly ghost-like. 'Look, I know what it's like to be compared all the time to someone else in your family,' he told her. 'I was always being compared to my younger brother, Josh. Everyone thought the sun shone from his one eye and the rest of the stars sparkled out the other.'

'And how did that make you feel?'

Liam didn't answer.

'Exactly!'

'I still . . . I still cared about him,' Liam defended himself.

'I care about Raye. 'Course I do. But sometimes, I can't stop myself from hating her too,' Nova admitted.

'And vomiting up every meal is going to sort all that out, is it?' asked Liam.

'I want to look like Rainbow.'

'What's wrong with looking like yourself?' asked Liam.

Quickly, Nova wiped her eyes. She stepped back and scrutinized him. 'Tell me something. What d'you think of my sister?'

Liam dropped his gaze, then turned his head. His beige-coloured cheeks had a reddish glow to them and the tips of his ears were a discernable fiery red. He instinctively knew he'd done the wrong thing. He should've looked Nova in the eyes when he answered her. 'I don't really know her,' he mumbled inanely.

Nova studied him before asking, 'D'you think she's pretty?'

'She's OK.'

'Liar!'

'All right then, she is pretty. In fact, she's way past stunning. Is that what you want to hear?' asked Liam.

'So why shouldn't I try and be like her?' asked Nova.

'Fine. Then be like her. She doesn't make herself sick after every meal.'

'She doesn't have to. She's so skinny, she probably has to jump about in the shower to get wet!' Nova replied. 'And I'm going to look like Rainbow if it kills me.'

'You stupid twit,' Liam hissed. 'That's exactly what it will do if you don't stop.'

'I don't care!' Nova shouted again.

'Oh, you fancy being like me, do you?' said Liam. 'You

fancy trolling around this hotel for the rest of eternity where no one can see or hear you? This isn't just about being dead, Nova. This place isn't just my coffin. This place is Hell. So go ahead, starve yourself, or give yourself a heart attack from all that vomiting. See if I care.'

Nova stared at him. With a sob, she ran straight through him, wrenching open the door to run away from his words as fast as she could. Liam stared after her, mentally kicking himself.

'Well done, Liam!' he muttered. 'Brilliantly handled. Well done!'

23. Nova

He knew. Liam knew. Someone knew. What was she going to do? Nova ran and ran, down the stairs and out of the house, and she didn't stop until she'd reached her favourite bench in the garden. She flopped down, gasping to catch her breath from all that running, and stared out towards the copse, watching but not seeing the last rays of the sun light up the leaves with a burnished gold. Funny, but she never used to get so out of breath, running from the hotel to her favourite bench. Everything exhausted her these days. The reason was obvious. But now someone else knew the reason.

What was she going to do?

But hang on . . . Maybe she was panicking about nothing. Liam was a ghost. Who was he going to tell? No one else but her could see him. But he'd got so angry with her, he'd actually been able to grab her arm. And when he got upset with Mr Jackman he'd suddenly become visible, right in front of him. What if he got angry again? Angry enough to materialize and tell her mum or dad what she was doing? Nova looked around nervously. Was Liam there, watching her right now but not making himself visible? And how long had he been watching her make herself sick? A month? A year? How many times had he watched her vomit? Nova shuddered with shame at the thought. It was OK when she thought no one knew, like a noble secret that was hers and hers alone. But now that someone else knew it didn't seem fine and noble any more. It was just shabby and horrible. Had he watched all her little tricks? Like insisting on peas or tomatoes or baked beans with every meal and always eating them first before anything else on her plate, so that when she was sick, she'd know when her stomach was truly empty? First in, last out. Did he know that she never ate chocolate? Not because she didn't like the taste like she'd told everyone, but because it smelt so awful when it came up again. Did he know about her having a fizzy drink with every meal, or oranges, or sherbet sweets – anything to fill her stomach with more acid or gas to make bringing up her food that much easier. All the little tricks and slips she'd learned over the last year, until vomiting had become more than a now-and-then pastime. Vomiting had become a way of life. A form of control. In fact it was more than a way of life. It *was* her life.

If things were going wrong it was because she hadn't got all the food out of her stomach. If she didn't do well in class, making herself sick was a way to make things better. And Nova knew it was doing bad things to her body. Her tongue was getting furry. Her breath now smelt so bad she was constantly chewing gum. She was tired all the time and any kind of exercise left her breathless and giddy. Look at the way she'd been left gasping for air, just from running up one flight of stairs at full pelt that morning. But Nova couldn't stop herself vomiting. She'd tried. But every time she tried to eat and keep it down, the food sat in her stomach like a boulder until she couldn't bear it any longer and out it came.

Liam didn't understand. How could he? Nova herself didn't understand. But Liam *knew*.

'Can I sit down?'

Nova didn't bother to turn her head at the sound of Liam's voice. Out of the corner of her eye, she saw him sit down beside her.

'I'm not judging you,' he said after a long pause.

'Aren't you?' asked Nova bitterly.

'I'm sorry,' Liam said. 'What I mean is, I didn't mean to judge you. I'm just trying to understand why, that's all.'

'It doesn't matter.'

'Of course it matters.'

They sat in silence as the sun sank lower in the sky.

'What's *your* secret?' Nova asked at last.

'Secret?'

Nova turned to Liam. 'You said we both have our little secrets. You know mine. What's yours?'

'It can wait.'

'No, it can't,' said Nova. 'Is it about Mr Jackman?'

Liam nodded.

'Is he . . .?'

But Liam began to fade out, becoming more and more transparent as Nova glared at him.

'Good way to avoid answering questions you don't like!' she bristled.

'Isn't it just!' Liam's grinning face was all that was visible before it too began to fade away.

'How nice to disappear whenever the going gets tough. Were you always this much of a coward?' asked Nova.

Liam's grin vanished. The rest of him didn't, though. His sudden snap back to opaqueness made Nova jump.

'How dare you? I'm not a coward,' he said heatedly.

'No? It's not the first time you've pulled your disappearing act at the first sign of something unpleasant,' Nova pointed out.

Liam glowered at her with a look on his face Nova had never seen before – and never wanted to see again.

'So are you going to answer my question now?'

'What question?' asked Liam belligerently.

'Why didn't you want Mr Jackman to leave the hotel?'

'He was planning to do something . . . stupid. Dangerously stupid,' Liam replied. 'He was going to explore the underwater caves in the bay to try and find me. And everyone round here knows that those caves are lethal. No one is stupid enough to go in them – especially at night – but m— Mr Jackman was going to try. I saw him writing an "if anything should happen to me . . ." letter.'

'You're joking . . .' Nova stared at him.

'I wish I was. He was convinced I was here even before he saw me.' Liam shrugged. 'But I think catching sight of me has changed his night-swimming plans. Although you confirming I was there didn't help get rid of him, which is what I wanted.'

'He'd already seen you and it was obvious he knew you.'

'But if you'd kept quiet, he might've thought he'd imagined seeing me.'

'Not very likely,' said Nova.

'But still possible.'

'Why're you so set against him knowing about you?'

'I want him to get on with his life,' Liam said quietly. 'I don't want him tying his life down and around me.'

'Why would he do that?' Nova thought of something. But it couldn't be that – could it? 'Liam, what's your surname?'

Silence.

'Liam . . .?'

'I should've guessed you'd figure it out sooner or later,' Liam sighed.

'So what is it?'

'Jackman.' The whispered word was all that was left of Liam as once more he vanished from sight.

24. Dad

Dad sighed, then quickly glanced up to make sure that his wife was nowhere around. He was in luck. There was only Mr Jackman hovering at the foot of the stairs. Dad glanced down at the computer on the reception desk again. He'd called up the month's receipts on his spreadsheet and it did not make heart-warming viewing. The hotel wasn't in trouble, but it wasn't far from it either. They just weren't getting the bookings they needed to keep afloat. Dad sighed again as he scrolled down the expenditure column. They were still spending too much and making too little. Cheap holiday packages abroad and the mystery that was English summer weather were combining to choke the life out of him. He had to come up with some way, some sure-fire way, for the hotel to make money. But what? Dad glanced up again. Mr Jackman was heading straight for him. That had to be a mirage for a start. Money worries were obviously affecting his brain.

'Hello, Mr Clibbens.'

Dad stared, totally astounded. Mr Jackman was actually talking to him! Flying pigs and blue snow would occur within the hour. 'Hello, Mr Jackman. Off for a walk, are you?'

'No. Not this evening. I thought . . . I'd stay in for a change. It really is a beautiful hotel.'

'Thank you. Yes, it is,' Dad agreed. What was this man up to? This was the most he'd said to him since his arrival.

'You must've spent a fortune on it,' said Mr Jackman.

'Every penny we had.' Dad hoped the truth sounded

more nonchalant than desperate. He allowed himself a faint satisfied smile. 'But it was worth it.'

'Did you have the place completely rebuilt?'

'No, the structure was still sound. But we had it gutted and completely refurbished. We moved rooms around, split some rooms in two, knocked some together, that sort of thing.'

'Any hidden staircases or secret passages?' Mr Jackman joked.

'Not a one,' Dad laughed.

'Shame!' said Mr Jackman, his smile fading. 'Secret passages conjure up so many images, don't they? Like memory mazes. Turn the next corner and catch the long forgotten scent of a dark-time dream or a daytime nightmare.'

'If you say so,' Dad said doubtfully. 'Are you into that sort of thing then?'

Mr Jackman shrugged. 'So how long did it take to renovate this place?'

'Over a year.'

'It used to be called Manor Hotel, didn't it?'

'That's right. We changed the name to Phoenix Manor – kind of like a new hotel rising out of the ashes of the old one. My wife thought of the name actually. But when she suggested it, I said, "Karmah, the name's a good 'un." And I was right. The name suits the place.'

'Yes,' Mr Jackman said, looking around slowly. 'Yes, it does. Well, I'd best be getting on.' Mr Jackman turned and headed for the stairs.

Dad studied him, unsure what to make of what had just happened. Maybe the man was finally mellowing out. And not before time either. 'Oh, just a minute,' he called after Mr Jackman. 'Talking of secret passages, there was one – well, sort of one – that was found soon after building work had begun.'

'Oh yes?' Mr Jackman was back at the reception desk in a flash. 'Where was that?'

'Down in the cellar, but it wasn't much of a passage. It stopped dead after about fifty or so metres and there was solid rock and earth after that.'

'Did you try to dig through it?'

Dad raised his eyebrows. 'Now why on earth would we do that? I wanted to rebuild the hotel, not tunnel under it like a mole.'

'Where's the entrance to this passage?' asked Mr Jackman. 'Is it still in the cellar? Can I see it?'

'I'm afraid not. It's kept permanently locked. We have a state-of-the-art wine cellar and storage facility down there, with some excellent vintages . . .'

But Dad was talking to Mr Jackman's back. Mr Jackman ran up the stairs, taking them two and three at a time. Well, so much for thinking the man was getting better. He was just as rude as ever. Dad turned back to his computer screen, then sighed deeply as he remembered what he'd been doing.

Money! How could the hotel make more money?

25. Nova

Nova just couldn't get comfortable. She tried her back, her front, then both sides – but nothing doing. She switched on her bedside light and tilted her alarm clock. It was past two in the morning. So much for sleep then. Maybe a glass of milk would help? Yeah, a glass of warm milk instead of something acidic or fizzy. And milk tasted absolutely foul when it came up again, so she'd be more likely to try and keep it down. And then Liam couldn't accuse her of not even trying to get better. So milk it was.

Wondering why she cared so much about Liam's opinion, Nova swung out of bed, pushing her feet into her fluffy purple slippers. She grabbed her matching dressing gown from the bottom of the bed before heading out of her room. The hotel would certainly be locked up for the night and the last thing she wanted to do was wake anyone up. The low-level lighting on the stairs and landing was more than enough to see by, but it was still strange walking through the hotel when it was this tranquil. During the day Nova sometimes had to fight to hear herself think but this was so different, it was unnerving. Pulling her dressing gown tighter around her against the cool night air, she carried on down the stairs.

She was on the top step just past the first-floor landing when she heard strange sounds coming from below. Peering over the banister, she strained to see who – or what – was making the noise. Then she tiptoed down the stairs, feeling strangely nervous, and leaned over the banister. The thuds were coming from the direction of the kitchen. It was probably just Mum or Dad or the twins up to one of their silly tricks – or Liam. It certainly wouldn't be anything for her to be afraid of. Liam was a ghost, for heaven's sake! And if *he* didn't freak her out, then nothing could.

Nova crept towards the slightly ajar kitchen door. A strange yellow light bounced on and off around the door. First it was there, then it wasn't – like a torch being shone around, or swung around. And then the light was gone. She waited for a few moments but the light didn't come on again. She pushed open the door. 'Dad, is that you?' she whispered.

Nothing.

No way was she going to go stumbling around in the dark. She switched on the light. The door leading down to the cellar was open and Mum always made sure she locked it at night before she went to bed. Nova walked across to the door and hesitated at the top of the stairs. The bad thing about the cellar was you had to go down the stairs to switch on the light. It was one of those things Dad was going to fix if he ever got round to it.

'Mum? Dad? Are you down there?'

Silence. But someone was definitely down there. The hairs standing up on the back of her neck told her that much.

'Liam . . .' Nova whispered.

But it couldn't be Liam. He didn't need to open doors to get through them.

'If you don't come out now, I'm going to get my mum and dad,' Nova challenged with far more courage than she was feeling.

A torch flicked on immediately. With all the light from it spilling forward, it was hard to tell who was holding it.

'The light switch is on the wall at the foot of the stairs,' Nova called out.

Still shrouded in shadow, the person moved towards the switch and moments later the cellar was flooded with light.

'Mr Jackman!' Nova frowned.

Nova and Mr Jackman regarded each other, neither of them moving, neither of them even blinking.

'What're you doing down there?' asked Nova, noting the torch in his hand.

'I was looking for something.'

'What?'

Mr Jackman didn't answer.

'Did you find it?' asked Nova.

'Not yet.'

'Maybe I can help you look for it?' Nova and Mr Jackman still didn't take their eyes off each other. It was as if they were saying one thing and talking about something entirely different – and they both knew it.

'I think you've found it . . . or should I say him, already.'

'You were looking for Liam in the cellar?' Nova wasn't quite sure she understood.

'Sort of,' said Mr Jackman.

'I'm not with you.'

Mr Jackman scrutinized Nova before speaking. 'I'm looking for an entrance to the tunnels your dad was telling me about earlier.'

'The tunnels? Dad had the entrance padlocked ages ago,' said Nova. 'And there was just one tunnel, not tunnels plural.'

'I was talking to Miss Eve earlier and she said there's supposed to be a whole network of tunnels running under this hotel and the grounds,' said Mr Jackman. 'If your dad and the builders only found one, then I think there must've been some kind of collapse or cave-in which blocked off access to the rest. And I need to find them.'

'Did you find the entrance in the cellar then?'

'Not yet. It's a big cellar and I'd only just started looking when you arrived.'

'But why? What's so special about the tunnels?'

'It's the only place Liam can be,' Mr Jackman said after a long pause.

'What're you talking about? Liam's all over the place. Believe me, I know. Nothing happens in this hotel without him knowing about it.'

'I'm talking about his . . . body.'

An ice-cold shiver shot up through Nova's body. Horrified, she stared at Mr Jackman. She'd never once thought about that. She'd never even considered the possibility that Liam's body was still somewhere in or around the hotel.

'I think that's why he's still at this hotel, why he can't leave,' said Mr Jackman.

'Who told you he couldn't leave?' asked Nova.

'Oh, come on. It's obvious. Why would he hang around this hotel otherwise?'

'Thank you,' Nova bristled.

'I'm not insulting your hotel. But if you had the choice, would you spend eternity in this place?' asked Mr Jackman.

Nova didn't answer. It was only now that the full impact of what was going on between Mr Jackman and Liam hit Nova. Mr Jackman was obviously Liam's dad. It explained so much. But wait a second . . . he couldn't be Liam's dad, could he? Liam was at least fifteen or sixteen and Mr Jackman didn't look like he was even thirty yet – not that Nova was any good at guessing adults' ages. Maybe Mr Jackman was really old but looked very good for his age?

'How did you know he'd be here in the first place?' asked Nova.

'I didn't. But this used to be one of his favourite places before your family took it over. I knew he wouldn't just disappear for all these years without ever trying to get in touch with me. So that meant only one thing.'

'That he'd died?' Nova whispered.

Mr Jackman nodded, his expression grim. 'That he'd died. So I've spent the last few years trying to find out what happened to him. If I could just find him and make sure he has a decent burial, then he might be able to rest in peace.'

'Dad's not going to let you go digging up his cellar and his gardens,' said Nova.

'Then you'll have to get Liam to tell me exactly where his body is,' argued Mr Jackman.

'I'll ask him. That doesn't mean he'll tell me,' Nova pointed out. 'I know . . . I know you're his dad but Liam really wants you to leave.'

Mr Jackman's mouth fell open. 'I'm not Liam's dad.'

'His uncle then.'

'I'm not his uncle either,' said Mr Jackman. 'My name is Joshua Jackman.' At Nova's blank look, he added quietly, 'Liam's not my son or my nephew. He's my brother.'

26. Nova

'Your brother . . .? But he can't be.' Nova couldn't take it in. 'Liam said he had a younger brother called Josh.'

'I'm his younger brother.'

'But he's sixteen at most.' Nova shook her head. 'You're way up there!'

Mr Jackman smiled dryly. 'I'm twenty-four in a couple of months.'

'Like I said!' Nova said, her point proven.

'Liam died over ten years ago,' said Mr Jackman. 'When he appeared to me he looked exactly the same as the last time I saw him . . . alive. Ghosts obviously don't grow older. But I do.'

'But . . . but . . .' Nova blinked like a dazzled owl as she struggled to grasp what Mr Jackman was saying. 'That's . . . that's . . . horrible. Poor Liam!'

Nova could hardly imagine what it must be like for Liam. How must he feel, seeing Mr Jackman and knowing who he was. Mr Jackman was Liam's younger brother, but now older and alive, while Liam was stuck. Stuck in the hotel. Stuck in time. Stuck like a fly in a spider's web. No wonder Mr Jackman was so desperate to free Liam – one way or another. Nova had assumed Liam had only been at the hotel for a few months, a year or two at most. And she'd never dreamt that he'd actually died so close to her home. Maybe even *in* her home if Mr Jackman was wrong about the tunnels. But to be here for over ten years. Even now, Nova still had trouble wrapping her mind around the idea.

'Will you help me, Nova?' asked Mr Jackman. 'Please?'

'I —'

'What in the name of ruddy hell is going on here?' Dad's incredulous voice boomed out behind them, making Nova jump.

'Ah, Mr Clibbens,' began Mr Jackman as he headed up the stairs to the kitchen. 'I was just talking to your daughter about the history of this hotel.'

'At two o'clock in the morning? Have you lost your mind?' Dad said angrily. 'Nova, what's going on?'

'I just came downstairs to get myself a glass of milk,' Nova explained. 'And I saw Mr Jackman down here and we just got chatting.'

'At two o'clock in the morning?' Dad repeated.

'I'm sorry. It was all my fault,' said Mr Jackman. 'I should've insisted that Nova go straight back to bed.'

'And just what're you doing down in my wine cellar?' asked Dad.

'I must admit, I became intrigued with the idea of the tunnels you were talking about earlier, so I thought I'd have a look and see if maybe there was another entrance to them somewhere down there . . . somewhere.'

Dad's expression was dropping in temperature with every passing second. 'At two o'clock in the morning?'

'I'm afraid, when I get an idea in my head, I like to go with it.' Mr Jackman smiled apologetically.

'At two o'clock in the morning?'

Mr Jackman shrugged.

'And how did you get into the cellar in the first place? My wife always locks up last thing at night,' said Dad.

'I'm afraid I picked the lock,' said Mr Jackman. 'You know, you should open up the tunnels as a genuine historical attraction. I'm sure loads of people would love to explore the route smugglers took centuries ago – and you do own the land around the hotel, don't you?'

'I am not going to stand here discussing real estate at two o'clock in the morning,' said Dad, his tone hard as stone. 'Nova, go to bed. I want to have a word in private with Mr Jackman.'

'But, Dad, we can explain . . .'

Dad turned to look at Nova and the look alone was enough to quell everything else she wanted to say. For once, she didn't argue. She'd never seen her Dad quite so steamingly irate before, not even when the twins had smuggled a live snake into the hotel as their new pet and it'd got lost in one of the occupied guest bedrooms.

Nova headed out of the kitchen. At the door, she turned to see her dad standing in front of Mr Jackman. 'Dad . . .?' she began.

'Go to bed, Nova,' Dad repeated softly.

Nova did as she was told and headed back to her room. She could only hope that Dad would give Mr Jackman a chance to explain. But somehow, she doubted it.

27. Miss Dawn and Miss Eve

The early morning sunshine streamed through the hotel lounge windows, dancing on the table where Miss Dawn and Miss Eve sat playing gin rummy. Not for money, of course. Miss Dawn didn't hold with such things.

'Things aren't going too well for the Jackman family, are they?' smiled Miss Eve.

Miss Dawn studied her companion, before she leaned forward to pick up a card from the deck. 'How sad to only find happiness in the misfortunes of others.'

'I just meant that neither brother is distinguishing himself at the moment.'

'They'll be all right.' Miss Dawn carefully placed a card onto the discard pile.

'Oh, Miss Dawn, wake up. Liam may be ten years older but he's not ten years wiser. He's still full of rage and resentment, anger and animosity, hatred and hostility.'

'Spare me the alliteration, please.' Miss Dawn was distinctly unimpressed.

Miss Eve sat back. Miss Dawn rearranged every card in her hand at least once, deliberately not looking at Miss Eve.

'Don't pin your hopes on Liam,' Miss Eve said softly, picking up another card. 'He's lonely. And his loneliness is clouding his judgement.'

'When the time comes, he'll do the right thing,' Miss Dawn said confidently.

'Not a chance. He's going to mess up. I can see all the signs,' said Miss Eve.

'Signs can be misleading.'

'Signs can show you exactly which way the wind is blowing. And by the way – gin!' Miss Eve said smugly, laying her cards on the table.

'We'll see,' said Miss Dawn, laying her cards face down. 'We'll see!'

Miss Eve asked irritably, 'Don't you ever get tired of saying that?'

28. The Eavesdropper

'To be honest, I didn't think you'd remember,' said Andrew.

'Are you kidding? I've been looking forward to this all morning,' smiled Raye. 'I even had my breakfast extra early so we could have a longer walk – but don't let it go to your head!'

Andrew laughed. 'I won't.'

He and Raye exchanged a genuinely friendly smile. They'd been walking and talking together for almost an hour, although the time had flown by. They'd walked around the hotel grounds and through part of the copse. Now they stood a couple of metres away from the cliff edge, looking out over the bay. Andrew tilted his head to one side as he studied Raye's profile. She really was quite a stunner. If only Kieran and Raoul and some of his other friends could see her. And, more importantly, see him with her. Funny, but when Andrew first saw her, he hadn't thought she was anything much. But the closer he got and the longer he looked, the better she appeared!

After a few moments she turned. 'Do I have something nasty hanging off my nose?'

Andrew laughed, but it quickly faded. 'Raye, you're not . . . you're not what I expected,' he admitted.

'Oh please!' Liam said from beside them. 'How long have you been practising that line with that sincere look?'

'What were you expecting?' asked Raye, oblivious to the eavesdropper who'd been with them since they'd left the hotel.

'A bimbo airhead,' Liam provided.

'Someone who wasn't as witty and pretty and fun,' said Andrew.

'Pass me a bucket someone.' Liam stuck two fingers down his throat, as he glared at Andrew. What a shame neither Andrew nor Raye could see him. How he would've loved to scare the living daylights out of Mister Fake over there. And those lines he was coming out with, they were straight out of *Cheesy Chat-up Lines* – Volume One!

'Please, kind sir, you'll turn my head.' Raye raised her hands to her cheeks and pretended to simper.

'You'll turn my stomach,' Liam muttered.

'Maybe we could still keep in touch after I leave tomorrow?' asked Andrew.

'I'd like that,' said Raye.

'So would I.'

Liam watched them, unable to think of a single thing to say to make himself feel better. In fact, watching the two of them together was making him feel worse. Andrew and Raye had spoken about school and their friends and their exams and all the everyday, so-called mundane stuff that everyone took for granted. At that moment, Liam would've sold his soul to be alive for just one day like them. Did they have any idea how much he envied them? Of course not. They had no clue about him. They didn't want one either.

'We'd better turn back,' said Raye. 'Mum and Dad will be wondering where I am.'

'Maybe we could take another walk this afternoon?'

'Sorry, I've got to help out before dinner,' said Raye.

'After dinner then?'

'I'll try but I can't guarantee anything.'

'I really want to see you again before I leave tomorrow. You're really something special, Raye.'

'You're laying it on just a bit too thick there!' said Raye dryly.

'I'll spread it a bit thinner then,' smiled Andrew.

'I'd appreciate it!'

'So would I!' said Liam.

Andrew walked at Raye's side, both of them oblivious to Liam, who was walking on her other side.

'Raye, don't trust him,' Liam tried again. 'He's a moron. He's just setting you up.'

Raye stopped and looked around. 'You . . . did you hear something?'

'No,' Andrew replied.

Raye shook her head and smiled. 'Just the wind, I expect.'

She started walking again. Andrew fell into step beside her. Liam didn't. He watched them walk away from him. 'No, it wasn't the wind,' he called after them.

The wind had more of an effect on how things worked than Liam ever did. He rubbed both his hands over his face. What'd he ever done to deserve the existence he had now? When was this hellish ride he was on going to stop?

29. Nova

Nova chewed her bite of toasted bacon sandwich until it was no more than watery paste in her mouth, before she allowed herself to swallow. Eating this way took for ever but it made it slightly harder to bring it back up afterwards. Slightly. Food that was only moderately chewed was easier to coax upwards. But Nova had to eat like this because she didn't want to vomit up her food, knowing that Liam could be somewhere watching or listening or both. It was humiliating enough knowing that he knew.

Swallowing at last, Nova charily placed the last piece of bacon and toast in her mouth.

'Nova, are you OK?' Mum asked gently.

Nova looked up from her plate, where she'd been carefully putting her knife and fork together so that they lined up exactly. Mum was giving her a studied look.

'I'm fine, Mum.' Nova immediately let go of the knife and fork.

'It's just that . . . you're so particular with your food these days,' Mum continued. 'And Raye and the twins finished their breakfast ages ago.'

Nova shrugged. 'I'm just a slow eater.'

'No baked beans or tomatoes today?' asked Mum.

Nova's face began to burn. 'Didn't fancy them. Can I go now?'

'Are you going to finish your orange juice?'

Nova looked at the glass. 'Better not. I mean, no, I've had enough.'

'Off you go then,' said Mum, gathering up the empty breakfast plate.

Nova stood up and went off in search of Mr Jackman, oblivious to the searching look her mum gave her as she left.

Twenty minutes later she hadn't found Mr Jackman – but she had found the toilets on the second floor at the back of the hotel. She'd tried so hard to keep her breakfast down – deep breaths, trying to think of something else, closing her eyes as she walked past any of the toilets – but none of it did any good. It was as if there was a line from the toilet bowl to her stomach and the moment she ate, the line drew tight and taut and pulled at her until she had to give in and follow where it led. So here she was, back in her favourite toilet cubicle. And this time it was hard to throw up – and it hurt. She'd had no orange juice to smooth the way back up. The back of her throat felt like someone had taken a grater to it and her stomach was aching. Was her stomach empty? Without her usual colourful starter, Nova couldn't tell. She retched again and her whole head was seized by a vice-like spasm so intense that her hands immediately flew to her temples. Flushing the toilet, Nova put down the lid and sat down. She closed her eyes in despair. She really hadn't wanted to be sick this morning. But her little ploys and variations in her eating routine hadn't made the slightest bit of difference. With a sigh she unlocked the door and went out.

Liam was leaning against the wall, looking straight ahead. At Nova's gasp, he turned to face her. 'You OK?' Stupid question! Nova scowled at him. 'Yeah, all right. It was!' Liam agreed, reading her mind.

'What're you doing in here? If watching me heave is the highlight of your day, then you need to get a life!' Nova could've bitten her tongue off. 'Sorry. I didn't mean —'

'Watching you upchuck is not the be-all and end-all of

my existence, no,' Liam interrupted calmly. 'Would it do any good to tell you I think you're nuts?'

'No!'

'How about if I asked you to stop before you do some serious damage to yourself?'

'I'm trying. Now can we drop the subject?' Nova said brusquely.

Liam shook his head, but he did as she asked. 'There's something else that needs sorting out. You need to warn your sister about Andrew.'

'Who's Andrew? And why do I need to warn Raye about him?'

'He's one of the guests here,' said Liam. 'He and his parents arrived yesterday. But Andrew was on the phone betting one of his friends that he can get Raye to snog him before he leaves tomorrow and you need to tell her.'

'Why?'

'Because Andrew's a low-life creep. You don't want your sister kissing someone like that, do you?'

'I don't care who my sister goes around kissing,' Nova told him, rinsing out her mouth over one of the wash basins.

'But Andrew only wants to kiss her for a bet. I tried to warn her yesterday but she wouldn't listen.'

'You tried to warn Raye? Is that when she saw you?' said Nova.

'Only briefly. A few seconds. And she didn't believe a word. All I did was cheese her off, I think,' said Liam.

'So you didn't tell her you were a ghost?'

'Of course not.'

Nova wondered at the feeling of intense relief that flooded through her. Why had she suddenly felt so anxious when she'd heard that Liam had tried to talk to Raye? Nova dismissed her worries. She was just concerned about

Liam, that was all. Raye would freak if she thought there was a real, live ghost in the hotel.

'Nova, you have to do something. Once Andrew's got what he wants, he'll have a good laugh at Raye behind her back,' said Liam earnestly. 'Now, I know you wouldn't want that to happen.'

Nova straightened up. 'You're more bent out of shape about it than I am. Besides, I've got something more important to do. I've got to find Mr Jackman.'

'Raye needs our help.'

'So does Mr Jackman.'

'Never mind my— I mean, Mr Jackman,' said Liam.

'I know he's your brother so you can stop calling him Mr Jackman,' said Nova.

'You two did have a cosy little talk, didn't you?' Liam said bitterly.

'He only wants to help you. I can't understand why you're so dead against that,' said Nova, bewildered.

'Well, he can't help.'

'He can if you'll let him,' said Nova.

'He can't do anything any more. He's gone,' said Liam reluctantly.

'What d'you mean? What did you do to him?'

'You need to talk to your dad, not me,' snapped Liam. 'And after that you can help me give Andrew Stanley what's coming to him.'

30. Andrew

They were almost back at the hotel and Andrew was sorry. He'd enjoyed his walk with Raye far more than he'd thought possible. He risked a quick look at her as they continued their easy pace, then deliberately looked away. He tried to turn his mind back to the job in hand. How best to get a kiss? But the bet made him feel uneasy at best and guilty at worse. Still, a wager was a wager and he couldn't back out now. And even if he lied and said he had kissed her, Andrew would still know the truth. He'd still know he'd failed, and Andrew didn't like to fail.

'I really like you, Rainbow,' he said.

Raye turned to face him, a ready smile on her face. 'I know! I've got something for you.'

'Oh yes?'

Raye dug into her jacket pocket and removed a gift-wrapped package about fifteen centimetres square. 'Happy birthday! I didn't have time to go shopping but I thought you might like this.'

Andrew took the package from Raye's open hand. 'You didn't have to do this, you know.'

'That's why I did it!' smiled Raye. 'Well? Aren't you going to open it?'

Andrew tore off the wrapping paper – and stared.

'D'you like it?' Raye asked anxiously. 'I did it myself.'

'Raye, I love it.' Andrew couldn't take his eyes off the present.

'I thought you would,' Raye grinned.

It was a pencil drawing of Andrew's face. Raye was a gifted artist but for some reason she had trouble drawing faces unless it was of people she cared about. Landscapes and still-life pictures were a doddle. And so was the human body. But not faces. But she'd drawn Andrew's face with a slight, amused smile crinkling up his eyes and curving his lips. She'd been up most of the night doing it and it was definitely one of the best drawings she'd ever done.

Andrew finally looked up, his eyes strangely bright and almost sad.

'Happy birthday, Andrew,' said Raye again. And she kissed him.

31. Nova

'Dad, where's Mr Jackman? I've been looking for him everywhere,' Nova asked.

'Mr Jackman has left the building,' Dad announced.

'What d'you mean?'

'I mean I told him to leave and he had sense enough not to argue.'

'Dad, you didn't!' Nova said, aghast.

'Nova, I did.' Dad turned to answer the ringing phone, missing the best of Nova's scowl.

Nova ran to the kitchen, then into the lounge in search of Mum. When at last she found her, Mum was chatting with Lorna, one of the two regular hotel cleaners.

'Mum, d'you know what Dad did?' Nova interrupted. 'He chucked Mr Jackman out, that's what!'

'Sorry, Lorna,' Mum apologized. 'Nova's manners seem to have disappeared.'

'Mum, this is important. Mr Jackman has *gone*!'

'Quite right too!'

'What?' Nova couldn't believe her ears.

'You heard me,' said Mum evenly. 'Mr Jackman had no business creeping around our hotel in the early hours of the morning, he had no business keeping you up so late for a chat about nonsense and he certainly had no business being in our wine cellar.'

'But that's not fair. He was only trying to find another way into the tunnels,' Nova pleaded.

'That's no excuse and you know it – and so did Mr Jackman.'

'How long ago did he leave?'

'I don't know. First thing this morning, I guess. If I'd had my way, he would've been out on his ear about two seconds after your dad found him in the wine cellar, but your dad persuaded me to let him stay until this morning.'

So it was too late to go after him. What was Nova supposed to do now? She went out of the lounge to stand in the hallway. Dad was still on the phone, taking a booking.

'Are you ready to help me with Raye now?' asked Liam, appearing beside Nova.

'No!' Nova said with belligerence. 'And why didn't you come and tell me that Dad had kicked your brother out?'

'Who d'you think woke up your dad in the first place so he'd find you and Josh?' asked Liam.

'You did *what*?'

'It wasn't easy either. I had to make enough noise to wake . . . me . . . before your dad even opened one eye!'

'How could you?' Nova stormed at him. 'Josh is your own brother. He only wanted to find your body.'

'Who asked him to? I didn't.' Liam glared back. 'I reckoned he'd outworn his welcome and luckily I wasn't the only one who thought so.'

'What kind of brother are you?' Nova asked, aghast.

Liam's expression gave her frostbite. 'Nova, even I'm not exactly sure where my body is. And I don't see your dad letting Josh dig around the hotel grounds for the next couple of years trying to find me, do you?'

'That's not the point,' Nova began.

'That's exactly the point. I meant what I said about Josh not wasting his life on me. Two wasted lives in our family ought to be enough for anyone.'

'Two?'

'Yeah, me and my dad. I'm not going to let —' Liam suddenly shut up.

'What?'

Liam pointed behind Nova. She spun round to see Dad, Miss Dawn and Miss Eve all watching her with a great deal of interest and, on Dad's part, concern.

'Nova, if you're going to crack up, could you do it in a less public place?' Dad frowned.

'I'm not cracking up. I'm talking to . . . I mean, I'm working on a new play and I was just trying out my lines.'

Miss Dawn and Miss Eve exchanged a look. Nova surreptitiously beckoned to Liam, then pointed to the front door.

'Where're you going?' Dad called after her.

'For a walk,' Nova replied.

Out she went, looking round to see if Liam was following her, but he'd disappeared again. When she reached the bottom of the steps, he reappeared in front of her.

'I can't get used to you doing that!' Nova complained.

'One of the few perks I get,' Liam told her ruefully.

'Don't change the subject! You were telling me why you wanted to get rid of your brother so badly.'

'I've already told you. I'm not saying anything else. Now, are you going to help me stop Andrew from making a fool of your sister or not?'

For the life of her, Nova couldn't understand Liam's attitude. What was his problem? He kept going on about how much he hated being stuck at the hotel, but he wouldn't do a thing to get away from it. All his brother – and Nova for that matter – wanted to do was give him what he wanted, a proper burial so he could rest in peace. Move on or up or out or whatever it was that ghosts in his position did. So why was he so against it?

'You're getting worked up over nothing. Andrew doesn't stand a chance of succeeding,' Nova said at last, deciding to put Liam out of his obvious misery.

'What d'you mean?'

'With my dad around, Andrew won't get the chance to so much as pucker up.'

'Don't you believe it. I know what boys like Andrew are like. There's no way he's going to back out of a dare now.'

'And what are boys like Andrew like?' asked Nova curiously. 'A bit like you perhaps?'

'You're jealous of Raye. That's what this is all about, isn't it?' Liam said icily.

'And you're jealous of Andrew. What's the matter? Afraid Andrew will get to kiss Raye and you won't?'

'That has nothing to do with it,' Liam insisted furiously. 'I don't understand you at all. Raye's your sister.'

'So what?'

'So if Andrew wants to hurt and humiliate your sister, you've got no problem with that? She's got it coming to her. Is that it?'

Nova glared at Liam. 'I never said that.'

'It's obviously what you think, though.'

'Don't tell me what I do or don't think!'

'Don't take your sister for granted,' Liam said softly. 'That was my mistake with my brother. I thought we had all the time in the world and we had no time at all.'

'Fine! Right! OK! I'll go and tell her,' said Nova. 'Happy now?' She marched back into the hotel, leaving Liam behind.

Happy now . . . Liam shook his head. Happy now? He couldn't even remember what happy felt like.

32. Rainbow

Rainbow sprayed herself with more jasmine perfume – a Christmas present from her mum and dad – and smiled at herself in the mirror. Andrew had really liked his birthday present, and been surprised by it too. Rainbow could tell. And they'd made plans to go for another walk after dinner. He really was lovely. Rainbow smiled as she remembered how taken aback he'd been when she'd kissed him. It was only a friendly birthday kiss on the cheek, but the look on his face! Raye's smile faded. He didn't think she was too fast or forward, did he? No! He'd liked it, Raye was sure of that. What a shame he was leaving tomorrow, but maybe they could keep in touch? E-mail or text message each other regularly?

The single tap at her bedroom door brought Raye out of her daydream. The door opened immediately before Raye could even speak. And in walked Nova. Raye groaned. That's all she needed, Nova hanging around while she was trying to get to know Andrew better.

'Did I say you could come in?' snapped Raye, throwing her perfume bottle back down on her dressing table. It clattered onto its side and began to roll slowly forward. She pushed it back impatiently.

'No, but you didn't say I couldn't either,' Nova pointed out.

'Well, I'm telling you now. Out!'

'But I've got something important to tell you,' Nova protested.

'Out!'

'It's about one of the guests here,' Nova began. 'Andrew someone.'

'Andrew Stanley. What about him?'

Nova turned suddenly to glare over her left shoulder before turning back to Raye. 'Raye, just be careful, OK? I . . . he was overheard talking on the phone to one of his friends.'

'So?'

Once again, Nova turned to scowl over her shoulder. What on earth was she doing? 'Andrew made a bet that you'd kiss him before he left tomorrow,' she said when she turned back to Raye.

'He did what?'

'He wants to kiss you for a bet. I just thought you should know, that's all,' said Nova.

'And you heard him make this bet, did you?'

'Not exactly. Liam did,' Nova mumbled.

'So we're back to Liam again? This joke you and Liam and Mr Jackman cooked up between you was tired when you tried it yesterday.'

Nova turned her head as if she were listening to something or someone. But if she thought that by acting crazy, Raye was more likely to believe her, then she was way off.

'It's not a joke. And Liam's not lying,' said Nova urgently. 'He heard Andrew talking to one of his friends on his mobile. The friend's name is Kieran. Ask Andrew if you don't believe me.'

Raye's eyes narrowed, her expression freezing by degrees. 'I don't believe you, Nova. One of the best-looking boys to come to this place in months and you immediately try and ruin things between us.'

Nova's mouth fell open.

'He likes me and I like him and you're just jealous,' said Raye.

'I'm stopping you from making a fool of yourself,' said Nova.

''Course you are. No wonder you don't have many friends at school. You're spiteful, Nova Clibbens.'

Nova tried her best not to look hurt, but she failed miserably. 'I'm telling you the truth. I was trying to do you a favour.'

'Out of the goodness of your heart?'

'Because I'm your sister . . .'

'Worse luck. Trust me to get saddled with a waste of space like you,' said Raye.

'Thanks. Thanks a lot.' Nova barely got the words out before racing out of the room.

'Lying toe-rag!' Raye slammed her bedroom door shut behind Nova.

What'd got into Nova recently? Over the last few months she'd grown very strange – sulky and secretive. What was her problem? She was just jealous because Andrew really liked her. How sad was that?

Someone thudded at her door. Nova! Right, she'd asked for it and this time she was going to get it. Raye wrenched open the door – only to stare at the boy before her. Liam again. Raye's expression altered at once. 'Oh, sorry. I thought it was my sister,' she began uncertainly.

'Hi, I'm Liam. D'you remember? We met yesterday.' Liam held out his hand, his expression anxious, almost fearful.

'Yes, I remember.' Raye nodded, trying not to stare. Liam really was lush! She shook his hand, wondering why it was so cold.

Liam snatched back his hand. 'Your sister has just run off in tears,' he told her.

'Nova's crying?' Raye said, surprised.

'She's very upset.'

Raye tutted. 'She'll get over it.' The moment the words were out, she regretted them. Even to her ears they sounded cold and unfeeling.

'I doubt it,' said Liam seriously.

Raye looked at him, before lowering her eyes. 'I . . . we just had a bit of an argument, that's all.'

'Nova was telling you the truth about Andrew,' said Liam.

Raye felt a chill feather its way down her back. 'How d'you know what we were talking about? Were you listening at my door? And anyway, guests aren't allowed in this part of the hotel.'

'No, I wasn't listening at your door, but I couldn't help overhearing some of the stuff you said to her and I can guess what the two of you fell out about. But I was the one who encouraged Nova to tell you the truth. If you want to take it out on someone, you should take it out on me, not her.'

Raye wanted to deny that she was taking anything out on anyone but the words died on her lips. She'd only met Liam twice and both times they'd seemed to get off on the wrong foot. Her face begin to glow warm with embarrassment. 'Nova knows I was just joking when I said those things to her.'

'Some jokes aren't funny.'

There was nothing Raye could say to that so she didn't even try. With each second of the silence that stretched between them, Raye felt worse and worse. 'I'll make it up to her,' she said at last.

Liam regarded her, then smiled. 'I'm sure you will. And I didn't mean to interfere in your business. It's just that I hurt some one very close to me once, and

I've always regretted it. And every day now I have to pay for it.'

'But Nova knows I don't mean anything by it,' Raye tried again.

'No, she doesn't,' Liam countered at once. 'She looks up to you and wants to be like you and every time you put her down, it knocks her confidence just that little bit more.'

'And she told you this, did she?' Raye frowned.

'She didn't have to,' said Liam. 'When I caught her deliberately making herself sick after breakfast this morning so she could look more like you, I got the message.'

'She did *what*?'

'And it wasn't the first time either.'

'I don't believe it. Nova's got more sense than that.' Raye shook her head.

'There are some things stronger than sense. Like the way Nova feels about you, and the way you make her feel when she's around you.'

'But . . .' Raye floundered to a bewildered stop. She couldn't take it in.

'You or someone in your family ought to know what's going on,' Liam said carefully. 'Nova's making herself ill by throwing up every time she eats anything bigger than a full stop.'

'How come you know all this and we don't?'

'I just happened to be around when she was doing it.'

'But . . . but why didn't she say something?' said Raye, dazed.

'You'll have to take that up with her. Anyway, like I said, I didn't mean to stick my nose into your business.'

At the sound of her perfume bottle thudding to the

floor, Raye's head whipped round. 'It's just my . . .' she began as she turned back.

But Liam had gone. Raye stepped out onto the landing looking left and right, but he was nowhere in sight.

33. Nova

Nova kicked at the sand beneath her feet. It arced up like a peacock's feathers before falling, some of it into her trainers. But it didn't stop her from kicking at the sand over and over again. She must've been mad to think that Raye might actually be grateful. At home, at school, it was always the same. Need someone to make fun of, look no further than Nova. Need someone to knock, to mock, to put down – Nova was available. It was like everyone looked at her and what they saw was someone dumpy, small, swotty, spotty – and that was all. Was everyone else right? Nova was desperate to change her image so that others would see her the way she truly wanted to be.

'You OK, Nova?'

Nova jumped, then snapped out, 'I wish I could just appear and disappear the way you do all the time!'

'No, you don't.' Liam shook his head.

Nova thought about it and decided he was right. 'I did what you asked me to do so please go away and leave me alone.'

'Your sister's really sorry for what she said,' Liam told her.

'Of course she is,' Nova said sarcastically.

'You should go back and talk to her. She's looking for you.'

'Why? So she can make me look like an even bigger fool?' asked Nova. 'Well, no thank you.'

'Nova, Raye really is sorry. I had a word with her and —'

'You did what?'

'I had a word with her and —'

'Who asked you to?' Nova said furiously. 'Why did you show yourself to her in the first place?'

'Because what she did to you annoyed me.' Liam frowned.

'But it's none of your business, is it? Just like you and Mr Jackman are none of my business . . .'

Liam got the point. 'Well, I'm sticking my nose in whether you like it or not.'

'Because you're burning to help me?'

'I want to help – yes!' Liam blustered.

'Why don't you be truthful for once?' Nova said scornfully. 'My sister's the one you're interested in, not me.'

Liam opened his mouth, only to snap it shut without saying a word. Nova took a deep breath, then a deeper one, but her blood was still boiling. 'Liam, please go away and leave me alone.'

Liam regarded Nova, perplexed frustration adding extra creases to his face. He slowly faded out, his expression, the way he was standing, everything about him letting Nova know that it was against his will. Only when he'd gone completely did Nova carry on walking along the beach, her head bent, her thoughts curling and coiling inside her head. Why did she want to be like Raye when her sister was so mean? Not to mention shallow. If Raye were a swimming pool, Nova would be able to walk from one side of her to the other without getting her toenails wet.

Nova sighed, knowing full well that it wasn't the way Raye was inside that she wanted to copy. It was what she looked like outside that counted. Raye made people's heads turn. And she knew it, but she couldn't care less, which made it even worse. And Nova had to admit, Raye wasn't mean to her all the time. Sometimes, she was asleep! But to be fair, she did stand up for Nova at school when one of the older girls had started picking on her. Raye had soon sorted that one out. And Nova had been so proud of her sister then. Until the resentment had set in that, once again, it was Raye riding to the rescue. And, once again, Nova was nowhere.

'Hi, Nova. I was hoping I'd see you down here.'

Nova's head snapped up. Joshua Jackman, Liam's brother, was standing in front of her and she was so lost in her own world, she hadn't even heard him approach. 'Mr Jackman! I thought you'd gone,' she said, relieved to see him.

'My dad is Mr Jackman. Call me Joshua.'

Nova wasn't sure about that. She wasn't used to calling old people in their twenties by their first names. She felt slightly uncomfortable about doing it. But he did say she could! 'OK.' She looked around. 'Does . . . anyone know you're here?'

'No. I dumped my stuff back at my dad's house and then headed straight back here,' said Joshua.

'I'm sorry Dad asked you to leave. That wasn't fair.'

'I'd have done exactly the same thing if I were him. I had no business being down in the cellar at that time of night.'

'And nothing . . . strange has happened to you while you've been on this beach, has it?'

'Strange like what?'

Nova shrugged.

Joshua regarded her speculatively. 'Liam wants me to go, doesn't he?'

Nova nodded.

'Is he here now?' asked Joshua.

Nova looked around. 'No. He was, but I told him to go. He . . . he won't be happy to see you're still here. He thinks you're wasting your time and your life searching for him.'

Joshua considered this for a few moments, deep creases furrowing the lines between his eyebrows. 'This is madness,' he said at last. 'I've been searching for my brother for so long. All over the country. Then I see him here, in a hotel dining room – and he's a ghost! I keep telling myself that I'll wake up in a minute and realize that I want to see him so much that I'm just imagining things.'

'I've seen him too, lots of times,' said Nova.

'But maybe you're part of my dream too. Or maybe I'm just losing my marbles.'

Nova wasn't sure what to say to that.

'He's really here, isn't he? At the hotel?' asked Joshua uncertainly.

Nova nodded. They stood in silence for a few moments. 'Do you have any other brothers or sisters?' asked Nova at last.

'No,' Joshua replied sombrely. 'Just Liam and me.'

'And your mum?'

'She died over fifteen years ago,' said Joshua.

Unsure what to say, unable to meet Joshua's gaze, Nova glanced out across the sea. Why was it so hard to talk about death and dying? What happened before and after death were easier to handle. Nova had listened to her parents and their friends discuss who was getting married or divorced or having a baby or moving house until their conversations rang in her ears for hours afterwards. Life stuff. All the everyday stuff that she and her friends and all the grown-ups around chatted about. And everyone loved to talk about ghosts and ghouls and things that went bump in the night. Nova suspected it was because not many people believed in actual ghosts – but they liked the thrill of being scared in a way that they could dismiss afterwards as not real.

But the subject of death, that was something else again.

Something to sweep under the carpet. Very taboo. Very hush-hush. Not pleasant to talk about. Not polite. Not nice. And look where it had got Liam and his brother. What had happened in their lives to make Liam a ghost stuck at Phoenix Manor and Joshua a slave to finding him? What was it that neither of them could let go?

'Where's your dad now, if you don't mind me asking?' said Nova.

'Where he's always been.' Joshua was unable to mask the bitterness narrowing his eyes and hardening his expression. 'At this time of day he's probably fast asleep. But his eyes will open at the same time as the local pub doors.'

'Where does he live?'

'The same place he's always lived. About half an hour away. Why?'

Nova was surprised. She had no idea Liam and Joshua's dad still lived so close. 'I just wondered. It was something Liam said.'

'What?'

'About two wasted lives in your family, which is why he doesn't want you to waste yours.'

Joshua turned away, but not before Nova saw the liquid sheen in his eyes. 'I need to find my brother,' he said forcefully. 'And I'm not leaving here until I do.'

'But how d'you intend to do that? The tunnels are blocked,' said Nova.

Joshua's eyes gleamed. 'Not necessarily. I've found another entrance, right here in the cliff wall.'

'How did you find it? I've been up and down this beach a hundred times and I've never seen an entrance to a tunnel.'

'I bet you've never been swimming in the sea around here, have you?' Joshua replied.

'No. Only paddling. The currents around here are too strong for me.'

'Well, I went for an early morning swim and I saw the entrance from about a kilo-metre out. Of course, with Miss Eve's help, I knew what to look for.'

'Oh, I see.'

'Liam's in one of those tunnels, I know he is,' said Joshua. 'I'm close. I can feel it. And no one, not even Liam, is going to stop me this time.'

34. Andrew and Raye

Raye checked both Andrew's room and the dining room. Dad said he hadn't left the hotel, so there was only one other place he could be. Raye stood in the doorway of the hotel lounge. Andrew was seated at a far table, his mobile phone pressed to his ear, his expression serious.

'Hi, Andrew.' Raye's voice was cool as she walked towards him.

Andrew immediately stood up. 'Kieran, I'll phone you back,' he said into his phone before pressing a button to disconnect the call. 'Hi, Raye. I was hoping I'd see you.'

'Well, here I am,' said Raye lightly. 'Were you just talking to someone called Kieran?'

'Yes, that's right. He's my best friend.'

'I see.'

'D'you want to join me?' Andrew indicated the seat next to his own. 'I need to talk to you.'

'OK.' Raye sat down; Andrew sat next to her and she shifted away from him slightly. It didn't go unnoticed.

'Is . . . is everything OK?' Andrew asked.

Raye looked at him, waiting for the right words to make it past the antagonism and disillusionment that churned inside her.

'Raye . . .?'

'Did you bet Kieran that you'd get to kiss me before you left tomorrow?' Raye said at last.

Andrew's mouth dropped open as he stared at her.

'Well? Is it true?' Raye persisted, unwilling to read the answer in Andrew's expression.

'Look, I can explain . . .'

'So it is true.' Raye couldn't remember when she'd felt so . . . so disappointed, not to mention disillusioned. Andrew was just being nice to her for a stupid bet and when Liam tried to warn her, she'd bitten his head off. And Nova . . . Raye groaned inwardly when she remembered all the things she'd said to her sister. She stood up.

Andrew jumped to his feet. 'Raye, I was just on the phone telling Kieran that the bet was off,' he rushed out.

'Of course you were,' said Raye, chips of ice flying from every word.

'It's true. I decided to call the whole thing off. It was a stupid thing to do anyway.'

'And I'm meant to believe that, am I?'

'It's *true*.'

Raye looked away, not wanting Andrew to see just how much he'd upset her. Her gaze fell onto the opposite seat, where her birthday present to him had been placed upright against a cushion. Raye's pencil drawing of Andrew's face.

Half the night spent working on it and agonizing over it and for what?

So Andrew could win his stupid bet. It took less than two strides to scoop up the picture and less than three seconds to dismantle the simple wooden frame she'd placed around it.

'Raye, no . . .'

'The drawing means something to you, does it?'

'Yes. Please don't,' Andrew pleaded.

'Keep it then. Keep it as a trophy to show your friends. D'you want me to write a message on the back, saying that I did kiss you? 'Cos I will. How much detail d'you want? Shall I say how long the kiss lasted and who had their eyes closed and who didn't? Anything to improve your sad, sorry little life.'

'Raye, I'm sorry.'

'Yeah, so am I.' Without another word, Raye turned and walked out of the room, leaving by the French windows which led straight out into the hotel gardens. She wanted to get away from Andrew and the hotel and her family and everyone and just be alone for a while. For a long while. She had to fight to keep her hands at her sides. She longed to wipe the tears from her eyes, but she wasn't going to give Andrew the satisfaction of knowing that he'd made her cry.

35. Jake and Jude

'All clear?' Jude whispered.

Jake peered down the stairs, looking left and right. The hall and, more importantly, the reception desk were deserted. 'All clear.' He gave the thumbs up.

He crept down the stairs, hiding behind each banister post in turn. He was Jake Clibbens, super-spy, the best secret agent in the universe. Jude slid down the banisters backwards, leaping off with a perfectly practised skill just before reaching the bottom to land on the bottom stair. Dad popped up from behind the reception desk.

'Jude, which part of "Don't slide down the banisters!" are you having trouble with, because I'd be happy to explain it to you,' Dad said, annoyed.

Jude turned an accusatory look on his twin brother.

'It's a trap,' Jake declared. 'Run!'

'Not so fast, you two.' Dad moved like greased lightning to appear in front of the stairs before the twins could get past him. 'What're you up to?'

'Nothing!' Jude said, with Jake nodding vigorously in agreement.

'Try again!'

'We're looking for the ghost,' Jake admitted.

'What ghost?' Dad frowned.

'Nova's ghost,' said Jake. 'The one she saw yesterday that made her scream.'

'She made that up,' said Dad. 'She just saw a spider and freaked – remember?'

Jude and Jake exchanged a look.

'Off you go and play outside,' said Dad. 'And stay out of mischief.'

'Where is everyone?' Jake asked, looking around.

'I saw Raye go into the lounge earlier,' Dad replied. 'And I have no idea where Nova is. She's like the Scarlet Pimpernel these days!'

'Who's that then?' asked Jude.

'Someone who used to help French aristocrats escape from the guillotine centuries ago,' Dad replied. 'But he was very elusive – which means very mysterious and hard to pin down – and the French authorities had trouble catching him.'

Jude and Jake turned to each other, their eyes agleam with the possibilities.

'Shall we play the Scarlet Pimpernel?' asked Jude.

'Yeah. Sounds cool!' said Jake.

'Er, just a minute, you two,' Dad said hastily. 'Remember what I said about staying out of trouble.'

'Don't worry,' Jake smiled.

'I'm your dad. That's my job!' Dad informed them.

The twins skipped off, grinning, leaving Dad to watch them, a loving yet rueful smile on his face.

'I wonder why Dad said Nova's ghost doesn't exist?' said Jake.

Jude looked at Jake curiously. 'Because he doesn't. There're no such things as ghosts.'

'Yes, there are. Nova's ghost exists. I've seen him,' Jake replied, surprised by Jude's response. And Jude didn't often surprise him.

'You heard Dad. Nova just made it up.'

'No, she didn't,' Jake argued. 'His name is Liam and he's about the same height as Dad and he wears jeans all the time.'

'What're you talking about?' Jude frowned.

'Liam. The ghost.'

'Stop winding me up. There's no such things as ghosts.' Jude's smile was hesitant as he regarded his twin.

Jake was just as stunned. He couldn't believe he could see Liam and Jude couldn't. There wasn't anything in the world that Jake and Jude couldn't do and hear and see together – until now, that is.

'You're just making it up, aren't you?' Jude said uncertainly.

Jake considered. 'Yeah, I'm just making it up,' he agreed at last, his fingers crossed behind his back.

36. Joshua Jackman

Joshua led the way along the beach away from the hotel. Nova looked up at the cliff face as she walked beside him.

'Are you sure what you saw was an entrance to one of the tunnels?' she said. 'It could've been just a big hole in the cliff that goes back for a bit and then stops.'

'You see that ridge up there?' Joshua pointed.

Nova nodded.

'The cave is just up from that. That's why you can't see it from the ground. It looks like a small, oval depression in the cliff face, but I've been up there and it's narrow for about a metre but then it opens out into a tunnel high enough to stand up in.'

Nova stared at him. 'Have you been along it? Did you see . . . anything?'

Joshua shook his head. 'It was too dark and I didn't have a torch or a compass on me. But I do now.'

'So you're going back into it now?'

'I've waited almost eleven years to find my brother. I'm not waiting any longer,' Joshua told her.

'But you can't just go in there. Don't you need all kinds of proper equipment?'

Joshua held up the rucksack he was carrying in his hand. 'I've got everything I need in here: compass, torch, spare batteries, rock hammer, rope, water. I don't need anything else.'

'Let me come with you,' Nova began.

Joshua shook his head. 'No way! You stay out here.'

'But the tunnels aren't safe. Liam said so.'

'All the more reason for you to stay put,' Joshua pointed

out. 'Don't worry. I've done this before. I know what I'm doing. Besides, I'm hoping Liam will show me the way – somehow.'

'What if something goes wrong?' Nova said desperately.

'Which is why I need your help,' said Joshua. 'I want someone I know and trust to be here in case I get into trouble. Give me an hour exactly. If I'm not out by then, you can go and get help.'

Nova was growing less and less enthusiastic about the whole plan. What had seemed fine in theory now seemed mad and, worse than that, dangerous.

'So will you help me?' asked Joshua.

Nova nodded reluctantly. What choice did she have? 'How're you going to get up there?' she asked, eyeing the ridge. It looked a lot further up than it had five minutes ago.

'Like this!' Joshua put on his rucksack and immediately began to climb up the cliff face, seeking out hand- and footholds with careful skill.

'Shouldn't you have a rope around you or something?' Nova called.

'No time,' Joshua replied.

Nova looked up and down the beach but they were alone. There was no one to help her talk Joshua down.

He was already halfway to the ridge. How did he intend to get round it? One false move and he'd plunge down. And he'd probably break every bone in his body – or worse.

'If you fall you could kill yourself,' Nova realized aloud.

'Either way, I'll see my brother again,' came Joshua's flip reply.

Joshua was almost at the ridge now. Terrified, Nova watched as he tried to swing out to grasp a handhold on the underside of it. Joshua had to swing his body out so that his entire weight was now supported only by his hands gripping scant handholds on the underside of the ridge. If he were to slip now . . .

Nova's palms were sweaty and, much as she longed to look away, she just couldn't. 'No!' She clapped her hands over her mouth as Joshua lost his grip with one hand. He scrambled to find another handhold, his legs and body still swinging freely under him. Nova's heart leapt into her throat and stayed there. She could hardly breathe as she watched him.

'Liam, where are you? Liam, please,' Nova whispered. 'We need your help. Please.' She didn't dare speak over a whisper in case she made Joshua lose his concentration. 'Liam, your brother needs your help. Please.'

Joshua was now at the edge of the ridge. He tried to swing one leg up onto it but he didn't swing high or hard enough. Even from where Nova was standing, she could see he was getting tired. He swung his leg up again, his foot just making the ridge. He pulled himself up using his arms and first one leg, then the other. Only when his whole body had disappeared out of sight did Nova breathe such a huge sigh of relief that she felt giddy from it. But it didn't last long. She glanced down at her watch. Joshua was about to go into a tunnel in the cliffs that would more than likely collapse down on him at any second. He'd asked Nova to give him an hour before calling for help but what if something happened to him before then? What if waiting that long actually cost Joshua his life? What should she do? She looked up and down the beach again. She was still alone. 'Joshua?' she shouted.

No reply.

'*Joshua?*' Nova yelled so hard she immediately started coughing afterwards.

Still nothing.

Nova went over to the cliff face. Maybe she should go up after him? Tentatively she began to climb. 'Nice and easy . . .' she muttered. 'Slow and steady . . .'

She was less than four metres off the ground when she realized she didn't have the physical strength to go any further. Her arms were aching already and her heart was pounding and perspiration kept running down into her eyes. She climbed down just as carefully, yelping when she caught her knee on a jagged piece of rock. She jumped down the last metre, wincing on impact.

'*Joshua?*' Nova tried again.

Panic rose up inside her like a tidal wave. Where was he? Why didn't he answer? What should she do now?

'Liam? Liam, where are you? I need your help,' she cried out.

But her only answer was the sound of the waves lapping up on the pebble-strewn beach.

37. Andrew and Raye

'Raye, wait. Please wait.'

Andrew was running after her. Raye could hear his footsteps crunching with quick regularity on the gravel. She carried on walking, quickly wiping her tear-stained cheeks. She turned off the gravel to cut across the garden. The dry autumn grass crunched beneath her feet as she tried to put as much distance between herself and Andrew as she could without actually running away.

'Raye, please.' Andrew ran in front of her, blocking her path. 'Listen. I was on the phone cancelling the stupid bet. I swear I was. It was a moronic thing to do in the first place, I realize that. I'm really sorry.'

'Why did you do it?' Raye asked.

'I don't know. It was just me, mouthing off. Showing off to my best mate. I'm sorry,' said Andrew.

'You're just sorry you got caught. Nova tried to warn me and I said some really horrible things to her—'

'Nova?'

'My sister.'

Raye hadn't spoken to anyone about Nova making herself sick after each meal. She'd dismissed both Liam's and Nova's accusations as ludicrous. But Nova had been right about Andrew. Suppose Liam was right too? Raye didn't even know if what he'd said about Nova throwing up after every meal was true – and that in itself made her feel at fault. She *should* know. Nova was her sister, for heaven's sake. It shouldn't take a stranger to tell her that something was wrong with her sister. Liam had to be wrong, he just had to be. But Raye couldn't do anything about his assertion until she'd personally spoken to Nova.

But she had no idea where Nova was or what she was doing. They used to hang out together, but not any more. When had that stopped? Raye took a good look at Andrew and knew the answer. Nova was too much of a rugrat to be seen with and Raye had made sure she knew that. Raye was nearly sixteen, a grown-up, one step away from an adult. Nova ruined her street cred. So Nova had been ditched, without a backwards glance. For people like Andrew. She didn't want what Liam had said to be true, but the fluttering wings of guilt in her stomach told their own story.

'Raye, I do want us to be friends.' Andrew brought Raye out of her reverie.

'Then tell me the truth.'

'About what?'

'About everything. About yourself. No lies and no lines this time.'

'I don't understand.' Andrew frowned.

Raye thought for a moment. 'Do you have brothers or sisters?'

'No. I'm an only child.'

'Spoilt?'

Andrew looked startled at the question. Then he unexpectedly smiled. 'Yeah, I guess so.'

'Your mum was a bit concerned about you yesterday. What was that about?'

Andrew shrugged. 'I broke my leg early last year and it took a while to heal. It gave Mum a chance to fuss over me and she hasn't quite managed to stop yet.'

'Oh, I see. How did you break your leg?'

'Showing off!' Andrew admitted. 'I jumped down from the wall bars in PE and landed awkwardly.'

'That must've been painful,' said Raye with sympathy.

Silence.

'I did better than the boy I landed on,' said Andrew.

Astounded, Raye stared at him. 'Is this a wind-up?'

'No. I wish it was. I broke my leg. But Julian was knocked unconscious. It was only meant to be a joke, but it went wrong.'

Andrew started walking again. Raye fell into step with him. 'What happened to . . . Julian?'

'He was unconscious for two days and he had to wear a neck brace for ages. We were both lucky that I didn't break his neck.'

After a moment's hesitation, Raye put her hand on his arm. Just that. Nothing more. But it was enough to make Andrew turn back to her, a strange defiance laced with regret twisting his face. 'You have no idea what it was like,' he said with a trace of bitterness.

'I can imagine,' said Raye. 'You must've been so scared.'

'Not for me.'

'I didn't mean that,' she hastened to reassure him. 'But you must've been worried out of your mind about Julian. Is he all right now?'

'Oh yeah, he's fine. Thank goodness.'

'And what happened to you?'

'I lost some of my friends. Invites to parties and days out dried up, that sort of thing. I was suspended from school – but then I was lucky they didn't boot me out altogether. I was the lucky one.'

'It must've been tough for you though.'

'I got over it. I got older,' said Andrew.

'And wiser?'

'Not as much as I should've.'

Raye nodded at that. They'd reached the hotel lounge again, without even realizing it. Raye suddenly felt as if she had the whole world on her plate waiting for her to deal with it, and she had no idea what to do, or even where to start. She faced Andrew and said seriously, 'I thought we were friends, Andrew. I imagined us swapping e-mail addresses and mobile numbers just so we could keep in touch. But I don't think that's going to happen now.'

'It was just meant to be a joke, Raye,' said Andrew unhappily .

'Some jokes aren't funny,' Raye shot back at him. How strange that she should use the very words Liam had used when he told her about Nova.

'Aren't you going to let me off the hook?' Andrew pleaded. 'I cancelled the bet. I promise I did.'

A slight cough to Raye's left had her head whipping round. They weren't alone. Liam was standing in a corner of the room, watching.

'Who're you?' Andrew frowned. 'I didn't see you when we came in here.'

'That's because you weren't looking,' Liam said easily. 'You were too busy trying to wriggle off the hook you put yourself on.'

'What did you say?' said Andrew incredulously.

'You heard me.'

'Who d'you—?'

'Liam, I want to ask your advice on something,' interrupted Raye.

'I'm listening.'

'Andrew here made a bet . . . but hang on, you already know this, don't you? You're the one who told Nova to tell me.'

Liam nodded. Andrew's eyes narrowed.

'Andrew says he cancelled the bet and wants me to forgive him. What d'you think I should do?'

'Tell him to get lost,' Liam said immediately.

'Who asked you?' Andrew flared up.

'Raye did – about five seconds ago. Or don't you have any short-term memory either?'

'Either? What d'you mean?' asked Andrew belligerently.

'Well, you don't have any class, that's for sure,' Liam told him.

'Why you . . .' Andrew took a step towards him.

'Just a minute, you two.' Raye moved to stand between the two of them. She turned to look at Liam. He looked straight back at her. 'You believe in speaking your mind, don't you?'

'Always have,' Liam replied. 'Sorry.'

'No. I like that in my friends,' said Raye.

'I'm glad you realize I am your friend,' Liam said softly. 'Because I do like you, Raye . . .'

'Let's see how you like this,' said Andrew angrily. He sidestepped round Raye to take a swing at Liam. Raye turned to him, trying to push him away. Liam ducked back, but not far enough. Andrew's fist reached his chin – and swung right through it. With a surprised gasp, Andrew tried to steady himself, but his centre of gravity had shifted and he carried on pitching forward. Liam side-stepped out of the way as he crashed to the ground like a felled tree.

'Andrew, that's enough,' said Raye.

'You . . . my fist went straight through you . . .' Andrew gasped.

'You wish!'

'Liam, please,' said Raye. 'Could you leave now?'

'I'm not leaving you with him.' Liam folded his arms across his chest.

'I'm telling you, I hit him, but my hand went right through him,' Andrew insisted.

Liam's head turned sharply towards the hotel reception and beyond.

'I hit you.' Andrew wasn't going to let it drop.

'You couldn't hit the front of this hotel from a metre away with a dinner plate,' Liam scoffed. But once again, his head turned towards the hotel reception. 'I've got to go,' he announced. 'Someone's calling me. Raye, will you be all right?'

'Of course,' Raye assured him.

With one last smile, Liam ran off before either Raye or Andrew could say another word.

'Raye, who was that loser?' Andrew said with belligerence.

'A friend of mine. And someone who tells me the truth,' said Raye pointedly.

Slow, burning red crept across Andrew's cheeks. Raye followed Liam out to the reception area. But apart from Dad and Miss Dawn it was empty.

'Dad, where's Liam?'

'Who?'

'Liam. The boy who just came out of the lounge.'

'You're the first person to come out of there in over ten minutes,' said Dad, returning to the mass of papers in front of him.

Raye shook her head as she had another look around. Dad never noticed anything unless it was directly related to the hotel. A marching band could stride through the foyer and out the back and if they didn't stop to book in first, Dad would never know they were there.

'I saw him, dear,' said Miss Dawn. 'But he's gone now.'

'Which way did he go?' asked Raye eagerly.

Miss Dawn shrugged. 'To the beach would be my guess. He's good-looking, isn't he?'

'Is he?' said Raye. 'I hadn't noticed.'

'Of course you hadn't, my dear,' said Miss Dawn with a definite twinkle in her eyes.

Raye's cheeks flamed. She went back into the lounge before the air around her head caught fire.

'Ah! How romantic!' she heard Miss Dawn sigh from behind her.

But as Raye regarded Andrew, she was feeling anything but romantic.

38. Brothers

'Nova, did you call me?'

Nova swung round, faint from relief when she saw Liam. 'Yes! Yes, I did. I've been calling you for ages.'

'I was in the middle of doing something, you know,' Liam said with frost. 'Something important.'

'So is this! Up there! Quick! Joshua's looking for you.'

Liam looked up immediately.

'He found a tunnel and thinks it may lead to where you are. But I've been calling and calling him and he hasn't answered,' Nova said, on the verge of tears.

'Why didn't you stop him?'

'How? Tie him to a boulder?' Nova tried to defend herself.

'Stay here. I'll find him,' said Liam grimly.

It took all of Liam's powers of concentration to think himself into the tunnels. He hadn't done so since the cave-in . . . Usually, all he had to do was think of himself at a place and he faded out of his current location and appeared at his new destination. And more often than not, he could move faster than a blink if he really wanted to. He called it tuning. Like tuning a radio station away from one channel and immediately to another. But thinking himself into the tunnels was proving difficult. He suspected that the cave-in was what had killed him but he'd never had the nerve to check and make sure. So since then he hadn't been in the tunnels. Not once. The thought of walking through them to be confronted by his own body didn't appeal in the least. But now he had to find his brother.

Liam closed his eyes and forced himself to think of the tunnels, to imagine himself inside. Nothing happened. Maybe if he picked a specific spot. He'd been through the cliff entrance before. You had to crawl on your hands and knees for a couple of metres but after that the tunnel opened out so that you could stand up. If he could just think himself into the part of the tunnel where it broadened out. Liam forced himself to concentrate on the tunnel and nothing else. He cleared his mind, then filled it with the image of the exact place he wanted to be. He knew the moment it worked. Even with his eyes closed he could feel the darkness. He opened his eyes and looked around, but he couldn't see his brother.

What was Joshua thinking of, coming into the tunnels like this? If he was so convinced that Liam's body was in there, didn't that tell him something, like how unsafe the tunnels were in the first place?

'Joshua?' Liam's eyes quickly became used to the gloom. The walls, the very air, were tinged with a bluish light which made everything around him very clear but very cold. Liam felt an iciness creep over his body that he hadn't felt in a long, long time. Everything inside him screamed for him to get out of there. Now!

But he couldn't.

He looked around again. Joshua was nowhere to be seen. Liam walked further along the tunnel.

'Joshua?' he called, even though he knew he wasn't in a state where his brother was likely to hear him.

Liam closed his eyes and thought himself another fifty metres along the tunnel. Then another. And another. With each reappearance, the tunnels sloped steeply downwards. Liam remembered that, from the cliff face, the tunnels sloped downwards for quite a while before there was a sharp incline towards the hotel gardens.

There was still no sign of Joshua. But the icy dread biting at Liam when he first entered the tunnels was now threatening to swallow him whole. It was like nothing he had ever experienced before – sick, blinding panic combined with a fear that gnawed at him from deep within. 'Joshua, for God's sake . . .'

Liam couldn't take any more. He was about to fade out and think himself back onto the beach when he heard a faint thudding sound. Just ahead, the tunnel bent sharply to the left. Liam remembered that the rise upwards happened just after this particular bend. At least, he thought it did. It'd been a long time.

It took all his powers of concentration just to stay put. Something about the tunnels, or in the tunnels, was zapping his strength. He could feel himself getting weaker. Maybe he should just get out while he still could. Being a ghost was bad enough. Being a ghost forced to wander up and down the tunnels and nowhere else because he couldn't think himself out would be an absolute nightmare.

There it was again – the thud-thudding. Liam moved forward tentatively. He stopped abruptly, taking a deep breath, then another. 'Get it together,' he told himself fiercely.

After all, there was nothing in the tunnels that could hurt him any more. Only his brother. Liam turned the corner to see Joshua sitting down with his back against the tunnel wall. His knees were drawn up as he stared straight ahead. His torch was still on and lay with his rucksack on the floor beside him. Joshua's left fist thumped slowly and steadily on the ground.

'Josh, what're you doing?' Liam squatted down to ask.

Joshua didn't move, didn't blink. Liam tried to touch his brother's arm, but his hand moved straight through it as if Josh were the ghost and not Liam. He tried to force himself to focus so that he could materialize, but it just wouldn't work. In the tunnel his concentration scattered like thistledown before a high wind. One thing at a time. What was Josh doing? Focus on that. Liam glanced down at Josh's hand. In that moment, he realized why Josh was thumping the ground. Pure frustration. Nothing more, nothing less.

'Josh, you have to turn back,' said Liam, hoping against hope that something of what he said would get through.

But Josh didn't move.

Liam looked around desperately. Further ahead, the tunnel was completely blocked from floor to ceiling. He stood up, horror like an alarm bell clanging in his mind. He stared at the rocks and rubble blocking the path. Instinctively he knew what was underneath the debris. Like a rabbit caught in a car's headlights, he could do nothing but stare.

Joshua jumped to his feet and moved towards the rubble. He took the rock hammer out of his rucksack and began hacking away at it like a man possessed. Years of anger and bitterness erupted out of him as he pounded at the barrier. Above Joshua's head, some of the rubble began to shift. Dust began to rain down from the tunnel ceiling. Joshua ran his hands over his hair to shake it off, then carried on digging at the base of the pile of rubble.

Liam sprang forward as more rubble was dislodged from further up the mound. 'Josh, don't do this. It's not safe. You're going to cause a rock slide,' he said desperately.

Joshua carried on digging.

'Josh, no.' Liam desperately tried to drag Joshua's arm away from the rubble. He made contact. His body was solid as he snatched Joshua's rock hammer out of his hand.

Joshua stared at him, stunned. 'NO!' he yelled, pulling away. 'You're not real. You're just a wish in my head, but

I'm not going to stop. Liam's here, I know he is.' He turned back to the rubble and started pulling rocks and stones and earth behind him in a frenzy.

Dropping the hammer, Liam tried to pull harder at Joshua's arm, but already he was dematerializing. Joshua dived to pick up the hammer before Liam could stop him and started hacking at the rock fall with renewed vigour.

'Stop it. You'll bring the whole lot down on your stupid head,' Liam shouted.

The rain of dust above them was getting heavier. Then came an ominous cracking sound. Liam remembered it. How could he have forgotten? That cracking sound was the last sound he had heard before he died . . . Joshua started hacking at the pile of rubble even harder than before, using his other hand to pull away the loose scree his hammer dislodged. Liam could see blood on Joshua's fingers where the jagged bits of rock had torn at his flesh. The cracking, rumbling noise was getting louder.

'JOSHUA!' Liam grabbed Joshua's arm and pulled him backwards. But not fast enough. A crack like the lash of a whip echoed around them as the pile of debris slid down like a rocky avalanche. Liam managed to pull most of Joshua's body out of the way, but not all. Joshua screamed in agony as his legs below the knees were pinned under a mass of rocky debris at least three-quarters of a metre high. Liam tried to pull him backwards, but Joshua screamed even harder and then his head and body flopped like a rag doll's.

'JOSHUA!' Liam cried out.

But it was no good. Joshua was pinned like a butterfly to a collector's card.

'Help! HELP ME!' Liam yelled.

But he and his brother were quite alone.

'Please God, no. Please, please . . .' Liam begged.

Gently, he lowered his brother's head to the ground. He had to get help and fast. It might already be too late. Where was Nova? Still on the beach? She was the only one who could see him no matter what. He couldn't risk going back to the hotel, only to remain invisible.

'Hang on, Joshua,' Liam pleaded. He tried to fade out and return to the beach, but he stayed right where he was. Frustrated he slammed his fist into the tunnel wall beside him. It didn't hurt, but his hand didn't pass through either. He had to calm down. But how, with his brother lying unconscious at his feet? Liam turned his head away, closed his eyes and forced himself to concentrate.

'Liam? Thank goodness. Did you find your brother?' asked Nova.

Liam opened his eyes. He was back on the beach with Nova right in front of him. 'Josh is trapped. Get help. He's hurt.'

'What's happened?' asked Nova.

Liam turned to her with such a burning expression on his face that he almost seemed to glow with it. 'Go and get help – NOW!' he yelled.

Without another word, Nova turned and ran.

39. Help

Andrew and Raye sat opposite each other. They'd been talking for the last ten minutes but they weren't back on the easy, friendly footing they were on before.

'Rainbow, haven't you ever done something you've regretted afterwards?' Andrew asked.

'No,' Raye lied.

'Then I feel sorry for you,' said Andrew, standing up. 'I really like you, but if you don't know how to forgive then maybe you're not half the girl you like to think you are.'

Raye sprang to her feet. 'Now wait just a —'

But before she could let fly with her indignation, Nova tumbled through open French windows, gasping for breath.

'Nova, what's the matter?' Raye ran over to her.

'It's Joshua. Mr Jackman,' Nova gasped, struggling back up onto her feet as she dragged air back into her lungs. 'He needs our help. He's in a cave . . . down at the beach and he's trapped. He needs our help.'

'Slow down,' said Raye. 'Where is Mr Jackman?'

'In a cave above the ridge near the old, broken boat,' Nova explained in a rush. 'Oh, please hurry. Get Dad to phone for an ambulance. I have to go back.'

'I'll come with you,' Andrew told Nova at once.

'Raye, get help. Quick,' Nova urged.

As Raye ran from the room to tell her dad, Andrew and Nova raced back to the beach.

Liam knelt down on the ground beside his brother. Joshua's breathing was erratic and shallow and his skin had lost almost all of its colour. Liam tried to touch his brother's forehead but his hand passed right though Joshua's head. 'Joshua, hang on. Help is on the way,' he whispered.

Joshua's eyelids fluttered open. He looked straight at Liam, but Liam knew he couldn't be seen. He was no longer solid. The tunnel effect again.

'Liam . . . you . . .' Joshua struggled to speak as the words fell out on a mere sigh.

'Can . . . can you see me?' asked Liam.

Joshua nodded. The movement of his head was only slight but it was enough. 'Real . . .? Not imagining . . .?'

'No, you're not imagining me,' Liam smiled. 'You didn't imagine me in the dining room either. I really was there.'

'. . . was so afraid . . .' Joshua's eyes closed.

'Josh, wake up. Don't fall asleep,' urged Liam.

Joshua opened his eyes reluctantly.

'Stay with me, Joshua,' said Liam.

'T-that's what I'm t-trying to . . . do . . .'

Liam froze at those words. He stared at Joshua in horror. 'You stupid fool!' he snapped. 'You may be older than me now but I'm still your older brother so listen up. I don't want you here, Josh. I'm dead. You're not. I wasn't a very good brother.' Liam paused and thought for a moment. 'I wasn't a very good son either. But I'd never forgive myself if something happened to you because of me. Don't you understand that? I couldn't bear it. I just couldn't.'

'But I . . .' Joshua began softly.

'But nothing! You don't owe me anything, Josh. And certainly not your life. I don't want it. And it isn't yours to give to me anyway.'

'. . . miss you,' Joshua breathed.

'I miss you too, you idiot,' Liam replied angrily. 'But if you want to do something for me, go out and have a life. And make the most of it – for both of us.'

'Dad's fault . . . shouldn't have quarrelled . . . with you . . .'

'Haven't you been listening to a single word I just said?' Liam raged. 'It wasn't Dad's fault. And it wasn't your fault – and it wasn't even my fault. It was an accident. I was unlucky, that's all.'

Liam stopped abruptly.

It wasn't Dad's fault . . .

Where had that come from? Liam had spent so long, maybe for ever, believing exactly that. Blaming Dad, blaming Josh too, if he was honest. But he didn't any more. His death was just one of those things. But life went on.

'Tell Dad it wasn't his fault,' Liam said slowly. 'Tell him, the whole point of life is not how you die, but how you live. Tell Dad I love him very much – and I'm sorry.'

'Liam, I . . .' Joshua closed his eyes and his head lolled to one side.

'Joshua? JOSHUA . . .' Liam yelled. 'Wake up. Wake up. WAKE UP . . .'

40. Andrew and Liam

'Andrew, you can't go up there. It's too dangerous.'

But Andrew was already searching the cliff face for likely handholds. Much as he wanted to just get going, he knew he had to take his time and work out each move carefully – or there'd be two people going to the hospital, not one.

Nova grabbed his shirt and pulled him back. 'You can't do this. For all we know, there's another ton of rubble waiting to rain down on the next person brainless enough to go in there.'

'Mr Jackman needs help and I can't do anything from down here,' Andrew argued.

'You could get hurt too,' said Nova unhappily.

'I won't. I'll be careful. Besides, I'm a trained first aider!'

'This isn't funny.'

'I'm not laughing. Mr Jackman might be in shock or worse and with no one to help him he won't stand a chance.'

'But Liam's in—'

'What about Liam?' Andrew said quickly.

Nova shook her head. 'Nothing.'

Andrew studied Nova. What wasn't she telling him? 'What's Liam got to do with this?'

'Nothing,' Nova insisted. 'Can't we wait for an ambulance and the coastguard?'

'By the time they arrive and get Mr Jackman out, it may be too late,' said Andrew. 'Nova, I'm not being a hero. Believe me, if there were some other way to do this, I'd be doing it.'

And wasn't that the truth. He didn't even like heights much. Without another word, he started up the cliff face. If he paused to think about the stupidity of what he was trying to do, he'd probably bottle out.

'What d'you want me to do?' Nova cried out from below him.

'Pray,' Andrew called back.

He breathed deeply to fill his lungs and steady his nerves. Keep climbing, he told himself. He'd be OK if he just thought of this as a climbing wall like the one at his local sports centre back home. He'd be fine if he took his time – and didn't look down. OK, now he'd reached the underside of the ridge, but how was he going to get onto it to reach the tunnel entrance beyond? He could try to swing along beneath it, but Andrew doubted that his arms were strong enough to take his entire weight for anything longer than a few seconds. There was only one other option. He'd have to climb past the ridge, then hopefully make his way round and then down onto it. He carried on climbing, getting higher and higher, searching all the time for a way to move across the cliff face so he'd be over the ridge.

'Where're you going?' Nova shouted from below. 'The ridge is to your right.'

'I know. Shut up!' Andrew called back, immediately sorry he'd answered at all when he lost concentration and slipped half a metre. Below him, Nova let out a strangled scream. 'Focus!' Andrew hissed to himself.

He had to do this. He edged his slow, careful way along to the cliff face, then worked his way down until he was about two metres above the ridge. Letting himself drop was one of the hardest things he'd ever had to do. Would the ridge take his weight? Would he even land on it properly? He forced himself to get on with it and let go before he froze completely. The ridge shook slightly on impact but that was all. And there before him was the tunnel entrance, concealed partly by the ridge and partly by gorse bushes.

Andrew ducked down and crawled in. It grew darker and darker as he went further in. He hadn't expected that. What if he got lost too? After a couple of metres the tunnel grew larger and Andrew was able to stand up, but the light coming from outside struggled to reach this far inside the tunnel. As far as Andrew could see, the tunnel carried on straight ahead. Taking a deep breath, he put his arms out in front of him and started walking.

One minute blended seamlessly into ten, until Andrew lost all track of the time he'd spent underground. He had no idea where he was and was beginning to wonder what on earth he was doing. After following the slope downwards for several minutes, he was now having to make his way upwards and it was hard work, made especially difficult by the fact that it was in total, inky darkness.

'MR JACKMAN? MR JACKMAN?' Andrew knew full well that he was not just shouting for Mr Jackman's sake but for his own as well. Nothing but the sound of his own anxious, shallow breathing was getting to him. The ground was beginning to level out now, but each step grew harder to take.

Deciding enough was enough, Andrew was about to turn round and head back to the beach, when something caught his eye – a strange, sickly yellow light up ahead. He stood still, wondering what he should do next. Taking a deep breath, he made his way towards the light. If it was nothing, he'd head straight out of this place before he became hopelessly lost – if he wasn't already.

A minute later Andrew was not just walking but running. He scooped up the torch on his way past, taking a few more steps before he reached Joshua Jackman, who was still out cold. Andrew kneeled down, playing the light over Joshua's face before flashing it around. And what he saw made him wish he hadn't. The mound of rocky debris before him stretched from floor to ceiling and looked as if it might slide and cover both him and Joshua at any second.

Andrew placed an ear close to Joshua's mouth and nose. Joshua was still breathing but it was shallow and erratic. He took hold of his wrist and felt for a pulse. Joshua's skin was cool and clammy and the pulse was so weak it was almost impossible to feel. Some soil and rocks from the mound before them slid down over Joshua's chest. Andrew brushed them off, forcing himself to bank down the panic firing up inside. He knew you should never move an unconscious person until paramedics or someone who knew what they were doing could check them over first – unless the unconscious person's life was in grave danger. Well, if this didn't qualify, Andrew didn't know what did. He couldn't leave Joshua. Any moment now, the pile of rocks and dirt would slide down to cover him completely. Somehow he had to free Joshua's legs – just enough to pull him clear.

Andrew carefully removed the dirt and rocks from Joshua's body, moving slowly so that he didn't cause a landslide. When he got to the rocks on Joshua's left leg, another pair of hands started removing the rocks from Joshua's right. Startled, Andrew fell backwards in surprise. 'You!'

'I thought you could use some help,' Liam told him grimly.

'Where did you come from?' asked Andrew.

'I came in after you,' said Liam. 'We can chat later. That lot is going to go at any second.'

Andrew agreed with a quick nod. Together they worked to free Joshua's legs. The rumble of rocks being dislodged made them work even faster.

'We need to pull him clear,' said Liam, standing up.

'One of his feet is still trapped,' Andrew pointed out.

'The rest of his body will be in the same state if we don't move him now,' said Liam.

Each holding Joshua under an arm, Andrew and Liam tugged at his body to free him.

'Come on! Pull!' Liam shouted as the bank of rocks and earth before them began to slide . . .

41. Joshua

'Wake up . . . Joshua, please wake up. Wake up.'

Joshua opened his eyes slowly. His head felt as if it were stuffed with cotton wool, but that was nothing compared to the fireworks shooting up and down both his legs. He groaned.

'Joshua? Thank God you're all right . . .'

'Dad?' Joshua turned his head to see his dad smiling down at him from the bedside. Joshua blinked wearily. Where was Liam? He'd expected to see Liam.

'You're going to be all right, son,' Joshua's dad smiled.

Joshua looked at his dad through half-closed eyes. His dad looked so tired, old before his time. Myriad silver strands now overwhelmed what was once chestnut-brown hair. What had once been a lean, wiry frame was now simply too thin. His white shirt and navy-blue trousers hung on him like extra-large clothes on an extra-small hanger.

'Thank God I didn't lose you too. I wouldn't have been able to stand that. Not you too . . .'

Joshua's gaze moved up to his dad's eyes, one brown, one blue. He froze in astounded disbelief to see the shimmer of tears.

'What happened? How . . .?' Joshua couldn't say any more. His throat felt as if he'd swallowed a ton of gravel.

'A boy called Andrew saved your life. Your legs were trapped but he managed to pull you clear. Apparently you stopped breathing but he gave you mouth to mouth as well. They're keeping him in overnight for observation.'

Joshua closed his eyes. He was so tired.

'Josh, I've got something to tell you.'

Josh forced himself to open his eyes at the solemn note in his dad's voice.

'They found a body buried under the rubble in the tunnel. They think it might be Liam's body . . .'

Shock, like a lightning jolt, shook Joshua's body. Even though he'd suspected as much, expected as much, it was still a blow to hear it like that.

'Where is he . . .?'

'They've brought the body to the hospital for confirmation.' Joshua's dad's voice cracked as he spoke. 'Liam . . . my boy . . .'

Joshua closed his eyes against the pain and grief on his dad's face. He knew his face held the same. But at least he'd found Liam. At least Liam could have some peace now. They all could.

'When you come out of hospital, I'll look after you,' said his dad. 'You will come home, won't you, Joshua? Just until you're better?'

Joshua turned his head away. He needed time to think. He hadn't lived at home since he was eighteen and had barely spoken to his father in all those years. But Liam said . . .

Had Liam said . . .?

Or was it just a hallucination? Or wishful thinking? Or just a strange dream when he was unconscious in the tunnel? Or maybe . . . just maybe it had been true and he really had seen his brother?

'My legs hurt.' Joshua winced. The fireworks going off in his legs were getting worse. He opened his eyes, just in time to catch the acute disappointment on his dad's face.

'I'll go and get a nurse. Maybe they can give you something for the pain.'

'Dad?' Joshua began.

His dad turned back to face him.

'When can I go home with you?' Joshua whispered.

His dad stared in disbelief. Joshua tried to smile but it came out pained and crooked. But it didn't matter. His dad took Joshua's hand in both of his. Joshua closed his eyes, fatigue finally overtaking him — so he missed his dad wiping away the single tear that now ran down his left cheek.

42. Sunday

Nova lay on her bed staring up at the ceiling. The morning light streaming through her window was rich and warm, but Nova turned away from it. Mum had already called her down for breakfast but the last thing Nova wanted to do was eat. If anything happened to Joshua Jackman, she'd never forgive herself. Josh was stable in hospital but his right ankle was fractured and his left leg was broken in two places. He was extremely lucky it hadn't been worse, a lot worse. Nova didn't even like to think about it.

What had started off as a fun game, a great adventure, had turned into something Nova never, ever wanted to experience again. She dreaded to think what would have happened if Andrew hadn't been on hand to help out before the ambulance arrived. He was the one who'd risked his life to climb up to the tunnel to help Joshua. And even though the paramedics had laid into Andrew for risking his own life, they'd freely admitted that if Andrew hadn't been there . . . And Andrew had been the one to insist that Liam was still trapped in the tunnels somewhere. After an extensive search, a body had finally been found. But when Nova had eavesdropped on the paramedics' conversation, she'd learned that the body was at least ten years old. She knew then that it was Liam's body. The paramedics reckoned it would take a number of days at least to identify the body properly, but Nova knew.

Mum and Dad had torn a strip off her for a solid hour once Joshua had been taken to hospital. As far as they were concerned she should have come back immediately to raise the alarm. And the guests had spoken of nothing else all evening until Nova couldn't stand it any more and had escaped to her room before dinner. She'd been there ever since.

And the very worst thing of all was that she hadn't seen Liam once in all that time. Not once. She knew he was furious with her. He had every right to be. He'd told her more than once that he didn't want her or his brother hunting for his body. But Nova hadn't listened. She'd convinced herself she was doing something . . . noble. The fact that she now knew better was of little comfort. Joshua was in hospital and Mum and Dad were furious and, worse still, very disappointed in her 'lack of judgement', as they put it.

A faint tap at the door made Nova sit up. 'Come in.'

To Nova's surprise, it wasn't Mum. It was Raye.

'Can I come in?'

Nova shrugged. Raye entered the room, carefully closing the door behind her. She looked around the room as if she'd never seen it before. Curious, Nova watched her, wondering why her sister was so ill at ease.

'How're you doing?'

'OK, I guess,' Nova replied.

'Nova, I want to ask you something,' Raye said, looking at her for the first time.

'Go on then.'

'Are you bulimic?'

No beating about the bush then. Just straight for the jugular. The blood drained from Nova's face. Her body went from ice-cold to burning hot in a split second. 'I think there are more important things going on around here at the moment,' she said.

'This is just as important as anything else. Are you deliberately making yourself vomit after everything you eat?'

'Who told you that?' Nova sprang off the bed to confront her sister.

'Is it true?' asked Raye, standing her ground.

'You're the one who always argues with Mum about food – not me,' Nova reminded her.

'Liam said that —'

'Liam?'

'One of the guests here.'

'I know who he is. And he's not a guest. He's a ghost,' said Nova grimly. 'It hasn't been confirmed yet but it was his body they found in the tunnels yesterday.'

Raye frowned. 'What're you talking about?'

'Liam's a ghost.'

'Don't be ridiculous. I'm being serious.'

Nova regarded her. 'I should've guessed you wouldn't believe me,' she said at last.

'Look, don't try to change the subject. I want to know if you're bulimic.'

'Why?'

Raye's eyebrows shot up. 'Because I want to know.'

'Why?' Nova repeated.

Raye shook her head at Nova, unable to believe the question. Nova walked over to her window. She looked out over the gardens and beyond, silently cursing Liam where two minutes earlier she'd been feeling guilty about him. He had no right to go telling everyone about her. No right at all. It was no one's business – not even Liam's.

'I should know,' Raye tried.

'What possible difference could it make to you, one way or the other?'

'I'm your sister —'

'By accident, not by choice. I'm just a waste of space. Isn't that what you said?'

'I didn't mean it.'

'Yes you did.' Nova's tone was matter of fact. 'When you're not insulting me, you completely ignore me. We may have the same parents but we're not sisters – not what I'd call sisters. You don't talk to me or share things with me. I might as well not exist for all you care.'

'That's not true.'

Nova turned her head to look over her shoulder at Raye. 'Isn't it? Be honest, Raye. Just for once, be honest.'

'If I didn't care, I wouldn't be in here asking if you're being stupid enough to make yourself sick,' Raye flared up. 'Since Liam told me that yesterday, I haven't been able to concentrate on anything else.'

'Am I meant to say sorry?'

'You're meant to tell me the truth,' said Raye. 'Are you bulimic or not?'

'Not.' Nova turned round. 'Now you can go away back to Andrew – or whoever it is you're sighing over this week – and leave me in peace.'

Raye considered Nova, a strange look on her face which dissolved into intense sadness.

'What is it?' Nova asked.

'You really hate me, don't you?'

'Of course I don't hate you,' Nova sighed. 'This isn't about you.'

'Isn't it?'

'No. This has nothing to do with you.'

'Then why do it, Nova?'

'And I've already told you —'

'D'you know what you're doing to yourself?' Raye interrupted. 'To your body?'

'You sound like Liam.' Nova turned back to the window.

'Nova, listen to me. I could help you —'

'With what?'

'Your hair. Some make-up. I could . . .' Raye trailed off at the look on her sister's face.

'So you're saying there is something wrong with me?'

'I'm not saying that at all.'

'Then why do I need make-up? And what's wrong with my hair?'

'Nothing,' Raye floundered. 'I'm just saying I could help you make them better.'

'Even if I wanted to wear make-up, which I don't, Mum wouldn't let me,' Nova pointed out. She turned her back towards Raye, wishing her sister would leave.

'I'm just trying to help.'

'Go away, Raye. I want to be left alone,' said Nova.

'Mum sent me to get you for breakfast,' Raye told her.

'There's no point in eating it,' Nova said without turning round. 'It'd only come up again.'

The silence in the room was deafening. Even when Nova heard her bedroom door open and close, she still didn't turn round. She had a lot of thinking to do. One thing was certain, she couldn't go on the way she was. One way or another, something had to change.

43. Realization

'I don't know what to do,' said Raye unhappily. 'She won't talk to me. She won't even look at me.'

'You're going to have to force her to listen —'

'How can I?' Raye interrupted. 'Nova doesn't want to listen to anything I say and I can't honestly say I blame her.'

Focusing hard on remaining solid, Liam took Raye's hand in his. He struggled to find something meaningful to say. Something that would make Raye feel better. She'd come into the lounge looking distraught and obviously seeking someone to talk to. It'd taken a while to calm her down enough to get her to talk to him, but at last the reason for her distress had coming pouring out.

Nova.

'I didn't want any of this to happen. I care about Nova, I really do,' sniffed Raye. And without warning, she burst into tears. 'I'm sorry,' she sobbed, embarrassed but unable to stop. 'It takes a lot to make me cry.'

'Don't apologize,' Liam said gently.

They sat next to each other on one of the sofas in the lounge. Awkwardly, Liam put his arm around Raye. She instantly turned into his shoulder, her tears flowing faster. Liam hugged her, feeling as if his insides were being flipped over — except that he didn't have any insides. Not any more. Once again, he wondered why he was still stuck at the hotel when his body had been found and taken to the local hospital. He'd thought that once he was found, that'd be that and he could move on. But nothing had changed. He had tried to walk away from the hotel, but

the same thing still happened. He'd collapsed unconscious, or whatever the ghost equivalent was, and woken
up back at the hotel again. Maybe finding his body had
nothing to do with anything. Maybe Liam really was
going to be stuck at Phoenix Manor for the rest of
eternity.

'This has been one of the worst weekends of my life,'
Raye sniffed, moving away from Liam in an effort to pull
herself together. 'What with Andrew —'

'I was wrong about Andrew,' Liam interrupted. 'He's
not the entire jerk I thought he was.'

'I'm glad, because I really like him,' said Raye.

Liam clenched his fists and turned away so that Raye
wouldn't see the look on his face.

'Liam, what am I going to do?'

'About Andrew?'

'No. About Nova.'

Liam sighed and sat back in his chair. He couldn't
remain solid for much longer. It was taking all his concentration to stop himself from fading right before Raye's
eyes. 'What d'you want to do?' he asked.

'Tell Mum and Dad,' Raye admitted. 'But that might
make things worse instead of better.'

'You can't just leave Nova to get on with it,' said Liam.

'I know. I know.' Raye shook her head. 'I need to work
out what to do for the best.'

Liam nodded but said nothing else. How strange! In
just two short days his whole existence had come to
revolve around Nova and her family. None of them knew
about him before. He existed around the edges of their
lives – with them but not of them. He'd convinced himself that he was fine, that he was OK being by himself.
He'd watched them getting on with their lives while he
had none. Their contentment in each other highlighted

his own sadness, their togetherness had forced him to admit just how alone he was. And that was bad enough. But now that Nova knew what he was and, strangely enough, he seemed to be able to make himself more solid more often because of it, his existence was surprisingly worse, not better. He grabbed a bit of life here and a bit of life there – but that was all he was allowed to have. And snatches of life hurt almost more than no life at all. Like just now, when he'd hugged Raye as she wept all over him. He'd have done anything, anything at all, to keep that one moment for ever. To have her company, to laugh and cry with her. To be real and needed by someone. When he was alive, in his arrogance he'd thought it would go on for ever. Now he realized he'd wasted so much time blaming his dad for something that was not his fault. Dad was hurting just as much as Liam was over Liam's mum's death. But in his grief, Dad had turned away and Liam had hated him for it.

Even thinking about Joshua gave him no peace. He couldn't even get to the hospital to make sure his brother was OK. It was too far away. He'd heard Nova's dad on the phone and although Joshua had broken some bones, he was going to be OK. But hearing it wasn't the same as being with his brother and seeing for himself. With a bitter start, Liam realized that just as Dad had turned away from him, so he'd turned away from his little brother. Maybe that was why Joshua was so determined to find Liam again, to turn the clock back.

Liam sighed. If only. If only he could have his time over again . . . But it was a pointless wish. It was never going to happen. But at least Joshua and even his dad could get on with their lives. They could move forward. Liam couldn't. He was stuck, watching the rest of the world go on without him. Stuck like a mosquito in amber. And he couldn't bear it any more. He just couldn't.

Liam stood up. 'I thought I'd go for a walk on the cliff top. I like to look out over the sea. Maybe you could join me?'

'I'd love to,' smiled Raye tentatively. 'If you don't mind my company.'

'I'd like nothing better. I'll meet you outside the hotel in fifteen minutes. I just have something I need to do first.'

'No problem. I need to wash my face anyway. See you in a minute,' said Raye.

Liam turned and headed out of the room. He was close to fading out. He couldn't, he *wouldn't* allow himself to do that in front of Raye. She believed in him. He couldn't lose that. He ran the last couple of metres out of the lounge, looking around quickly before he let himself go. He was safe. There was only Miss Dawn deep in conversation with Raye's mum at the reception desk. But as he began to fade out, Miss Dawn turned to look directly at him.

She had the saddest look on her face he'd ever seen. And she wasn't sad for herself. Liam instinctively realized that she was deeply sad for him. Before he disappeared altogether he had the strangest feeling that, in some way he didn't begin to understand, she was desperately worried.

44. Liam

'Well?'

Nova put her hand over the mouthpiece. 'Just a minute!' she hissed at Liam.

They were in the tiny private study that Mum and Dad used as their office. It was the only place where they could use a phone undisturbed.

'I'm sorry,' said the voice at the other end of the phone, 'but we can only give out that kind of information to members of the immediate family.'

'I just want to know how he's doing,' Nova pleaded.

Liam was almost jigging up and down in front of her. He moved to get his ear as close to the phone as possible.

'I'm sorry,' the male nurse told Nova. 'It's against hospital policy.'

Nova sighed. 'Thanks anyway.' She put down the phone. 'Well, I tried.'

No way was that the end of it. Liam wasn't going to stop at the first hurdle. He just had to think. Focus and think. 'I'm not giving up now,' he said, his lips set.

Then he had a brilliant idea. If he could just persuade Nova to . . .

'I'm not going to the hospital to find out how your brother is doing, so forget it,' said Nova hastily.

'Did I ask you to?' Liam snapped, because that was just what he was going to ask her to do. 'And I'd have thought you'd be only too glad to help me, as this is all your fault in the first place.'

Nova dredged up the filthiest look she had and let Liam have it, full force. Head high, she went to march past him.

'I'm sorry,' Liam told her.

Nova carried on walking. Liam ran round her to stand in her way. He wasn't surprised she was annoyed. What was the matter with him? Why did he always need someone to blame?

'I'm really sorry. I shouldn't have said that,' said Liam.

'If that's what you really believe, why not?' Nova said frostily.

'Of course I don't believe it. It's not anyone's fault. And I'm sorry. I . . . I'm just not sure which way is up at the moment. OK?'

'OK,' Nova said at last. 'But there was no need to bite my head off. I am doing my best.'

'Yes, I know. Thank you.'

'Not that my best has got us very far,' she sighed.

'Hmm!' Liam agreed, his tone morose, his head bent. Suddenly he looked at Nova, his eyes lit up. 'My dad! Phone my dad.'

Nova caught on immediately. 'Will your dad tell me how Mr— I mean, Joshua is doing?'

'I'll tell you what to say,' said Liam.

Nova moved back to the phone. 'D'you know what his number is?'

Liam considered. 'Probably the same as when I lived there with him. He's in the same house we've always lived in, so why would he change it? And if he has, we'll phone directory enquiries.'

Nova keyed in the number Liam gave her. Her mouth was dry, her throat tight as she waited to see if anyone picked up the phone at the other end.

'Hello?'

'Hello? Mr Jackman?' said Nova breathlessly.

'Yes . . .?'

'Ask him about Joshua,' Liam whispered.

'Mr Jackman, I'm a . . . friend of your son, Joshua. I was just phoning to find out how he's doing.'

Liam moved to stand on the other side of the phone so that he could also hear the conversation.

'He's stable in hospital. I'm just on my way to see him now,' said Mr Jackman.

A jolt like lightning shot through Liam. His dad's voice. His dad was at the other end of that phone line. How was he? Did he look the same? Had he changed? Was he missing Liam — as much as Liam was missing him? Liam closed his eyes, feeling his throat get tighter and his eyes begin to well up. How stupid to cry at the sound of his dad's voice. He hadn't cried like that before. Why start now?

'Joshua's going to be all right, isn't he?' asked Nova.

'His legs will take a while to heal but luckily he didn't have to wait too long for help to arrive,' said Mr Jackman. 'Who is this?'

'My name is Nova. Nova Clibbens from the Phoenix Manor Hotel.'

'I understand my son was staying there for a while,' said Mr Jackman.

'That's right.' Nova was about to add more but then she thought better of it.

'You were one of the ones who found him, weren't you?'

'I suppose so. And I was on the beach when the ambulance arrived.' Nova didn't want to take credit where she deserved none. 'I didn't do much.'

'Thank you. I'm afraid they're just small, very inadequate words, but thank you so much,' said Mr Jackman. 'I won't forget it.'

'That's OK,' said Nova, feeling distinctly uncomfortable.

Liam smiled at her. He knew what she was going

through, but the last thing she needed now was to blame herself for what had happened to his brother.

'When Joshua gets out of hospital, you're more than welcome to visit him if you want to.'

'Thank you,' said Nova. 'But I thought he lived in Manchester.'

'My son will be staying with me for a while,' said Mr Jackman firmly. 'I'll be looking after him.'

Liam straightened up and turned away, but not before Nova saw the odd expression on his face. He looked . . . hurt.

'Well, thanks for letting me know about Joshua,' said Nova. 'Please tell him that I hope he gets better soon.'

After the goodbyes had been said Nova slowly put down the phone. She walked round Liam to look directly at him. 'What's the matter?'

'Nothing.'

'Your brother's going to be fine.'

'I heard,' said Liam. 'And he's going to recuperate at Dad's.'

'That's good news, at any rate,' said Nova.

Liam didn't answer.

'Isn't it?' prompted Nova, puzzled.

Liam still didn't answer.

'I thought that's what you wanted, for Joshua to get on with his life and maybe get back together with your dad?'

'It was . . . it is.'

'Then why the face?'

'I don't know what you mean.'

'Rubbish! Your face is longer than a physics exam. Aren't you happy for them?'

'Yeah, it's great that they've got together again. But what about me?' Liam suddenly flared up. 'Where does that leave me? I can't think myself into Dad's house any more than I can visit Josh in hospital. I can't get further than a mile in any direction.'

'You can still stay here—' Nova began.

'By myself. Watching you and your family and your guests get on with their lives. Watching all of you grow up, move out, move on – while I'm still stuck here like . . . like bad wallpaper.'

What could Nova say to that? She stared, stricken, at Liam, obviously feeling bad for him. Liam glared at her, hating that sympathetic look on her face. He didn't want her pity. How dare she?

'Or are you going to starve yourself to death so you can be with me for all time?' Liam asked viciously.

'That's . . . that's horrible,' Nova gasped.

'Is it? You're the one throwing up your food. You're the one who has a choice in this and you're choosing to die—'

'No, I'm not!' Nova yelled at him. 'I want to be thin. I want to look like Rainbow. I don't want to die. That's a terrible thing to say.'

'What does it matter if you're thin or fat?' asked Liam. 'There are worse things in this world to be, you know.'

'You don't understand—'

'No, I don't. And I don't want to. On a scale of one to ten, your problems don't even make the chart,' said Liam. 'I'm alone. This time tomorrow I'll be alone and this time next year and this time in the next century, I'll probably still be stuck here.'

'That's not my fault.'

'I never said it was.'

'Then why're you taking it out on me? If you really want to move on, then do something about it. Find a way. Let me help you.'

'I don't want your help.'

'Oh, that's right. You don't need anyone's help, do you? You want to stay here whingeing about your life but you won't help yourself and you won't let anyone else help you either.'

'In case you haven't noticed, I haven't got a life to whine about,' said Liam.

'I'm serious, Liam. If you won't help yourself then you've got no one else to blame for where you are now,' said Nova.

'And the same goes for you,' Liam told her succinctly.

Nova stared at him. Liam could tell that she understood immediately what he was talking about and she didn't like it one little bit. 'You know something,' he said softly. 'Maybe I should've left you and Joshua and Andrew to it. Maybe I should've let you get yourselves killed. Then at least I would've had some company.'

'You don't mean that,' Nova said, aghast.

'Don't I? I just spent the last decade by myself, Nova. I don't intend to do the same for the rest of eternity.'

'What're you going to do?' asked Nova, a frisson of fear chilling her entire body.

'I can't be by myself again, Nova. I just can't,' said Liam. 'And if that means doing something that's going to make you hate me – and make me hate myself – then so be it.'

'What're you talking about?' The alarm bells pealing inside her were deafening.

Liam didn't say a word as he slowly began to fade out.

'Answer me,' Nova ordered desperately. 'Liam, where're you going?'

'I've got to meet someone.'

'Who?'

'No one you know.'

'Liam . . .? Come back. Liam . . .?'

Liam could hear her voice echoing after him, but he didn't go back. He was so desperately tired of being lonely. He was just so desperately tired. He had meant every word of what he'd just said – and it scared him.

But being alone scared him even more.

45. Confession

'Isn't it terrible about the man trapped in one of the tunnels around here?' said Mrs Cooper, the elderly woman at the reception desk. 'The guard on our train told us all about it.'

'Yes, it was terrible,' Dad agreed. 'Thank goodness he was found in time.'

'And I understand a body was found in the tunnels. A body that's centuries old.' Mr Cooper's blue eyes gleamed.

'I'm not sure it's centuries old. They did find a body and it's been taken away for further analysis,' Dad informed them. 'But most people round here think it's the body of a boy who disappeared over ten years ago.'

'Is there any chance that we might have a quick look in the tunnels?' asked Mrs Cooper hopefully.

'You're the seventh person today to ask me that.' Dad's smile took the edge off his words. 'I'm afraid I couldn't possibly let anyone into the tunnels while they're so unsafe.'

'What a shame!' Mrs Cooper was extremely disappointed.

'Do you plan to open them once they have been made safe?' asked Mr Cooper.

'I'm not sure. Maybe,' said Dad truthfully. 'Anyway, you said you'd like a room for how many days?'

'Dad, where's Raye?' asked Nova.

'Nova, I'm trying to book these people in.' Dad smiled through gritted teeth.

'This is important,' said Nova. 'I have to talk to her.'

Nova had spent the last twenty minutes sitting in the hotel lounge trying to make up her mind what she should do next. Now she'd finally decided to talk to Raye. She'd tell her sister the truth about her bingeing and vomiting – and the reasons behind it – and if Raye decided to tell Mum and Dad then so be it. And Nova was going to tell Raye about Liam – all about him. She'd sit Raye down and make her listen and she wouldn't stop until Raye believed her. In his current mood, there was no telling what Liam might do and Nova felt totally out of her depth. But Liam really liked Raye. If he was going to listen to anyone, it would be her sister.

'Raye said she was going for a walk,' said Dad, less than impressed with Nova's interruption.

'Where?'

'I'm so sorry. I'll only be a moment,' Dad apologized to the elderly man and woman waiting to check in.

'Take your time, dear,' the elderly woman smiled.

'She went to the cliffs. Or the beach,' Dad said to Nova impatiently. 'She said she was meeting a friend there.'

'Who? Is Andrew out of hospital then?'

'I'm not sure. Maybe. Now if you don't mind . . .'

'Why is she going for a walk?' asked Nova.

'Because it's a lovely day? Because there's an R in the month? Take it up with your sister. OK?' said Dad, adding to himself, 'I'll be glad when school starts again!'

With a deep frown turning down every line in her face, Nova headed into the kitchen.

'Hello, love,' said Mum, placing a huge roasting tray filled with marinated chicken portions in the oven. 'Come for a snack?'

'No, I . . . Mum, can I talk to you?' said Nova.

Mum shut the oven door and sat down at the table. To Nova's surprise, she instantly had her mum's full attention.

Mum's expression was watchful as she indicated the chair opposite her. Nova sat down.

'What is it, Mum?' asked Nova.

'I should be asking you that. I've thought for some time that maybe you had something to tell me,' said Mum gently.

'Like what?'

'I don't know, Nova,' said Mum. 'But something's going on with you, isn't it?'

Nova nodded.

'Is it school?' Mum asked at last when Nova didn't continue.

Nova shook her head.

'Are you being bullied?'

'No, nothing like that,' said Nova.

'Then I'll shut up and let you tell me,' smiled Mum.

'I was really going to talk to Raye about this first,' Nova began.

'Anything you can tell Raye, you can tell me,' said Mum quietly. 'But I'm glad to see you two are friends again. You both had me worried there for a while.'

'Why?'

'Well, it was like you weren't sisters and you weren't friends. Like you didn't even know each other any more . . . So what is it you want to tell me?'

'You won't like it,' Nova sighed.

'I rather thought I wouldn't,' said Mum.

'It's just that . . .' The alarm bells that had been pealing in Nova's head a while ago now sounded as loud as cannon fire. Why was that phrase so familiar – 'like you didn't even know each other any more . . .'? Where had she just heard something similar? Like a light being switched on in her head, Nova suddenly remembered. She sprang up from the table. 'Raye's meeting Liam . . .' she said, appalled.

Mum sat back in her chair. 'Is that what you wanted to tell me? Raye's gone for a walk with her latest boyfriend?'

'No, I . . . Mum, I've got to go,' said Nova, already on the way to the door.

'But what about our talk?'

'We'll talk later, I promise.'

'Nova . . .?'

'I promise, Mum,' Nova said earnestly. 'But I've got to find Raye before it's too late.'

'Before what's too late? Nova?'

But Nova was gone.

46. The Final Test

Liam and Raye walked along the cliff top in a comfortable silence. Liam had listened to Raye chat about life at the hotel for the last ten minutes and it'd felt great to have a proper conversation again. The strange thing was, now he was outside, he didn't feel even close to fading out. He supposed it was because he was still too keyed up after his talk with Nova. Or maybe it was simply that he wanted to be here with Raye more than anything else in the world.

'I'm sorry I didn't believe you about Nova. You were right all along,' Raye said unexpectedly. 'She is . . . ill at the moment.'

'I don't think she sees it as an illness,' said Liam.

'But it is – right? I mean, she's deliberately making herself sick.'

'Did she tell you that?' Liam asked, surprised.

'Yes . . . no . . . not in so many words, but I could tell,' said Raye. 'I feel like it's all my fault.'

'It's not your fault, it's not Nova's fault. It's just one of those things you all have to get on and deal with.'

'We used to be close, you know – Nova and me. I didn't realize how far we'd grown apart until I asked her about her . . . bulimia. She wouldn't look at me and I stood in her bedroom realizing that I didn't really know my sister any more. Does that make sense?'

Liam nodded.

'It was so strange. It was like looking at a stranger. I feel closer to you at the moment than I do to my own sister – if you see what I mean.' Raye's cheeks took on a reddish tinge as she looked away, embarrassed. 'Am I talking too much?'

'No, not at all,' Liam hurried to reassure her. 'Besides, I like to listen to you.'

'You're the first one who does!' Raye smiled.

Liam returned her smile and looked out over the sea towards the horizon. This was the happiest he'd been in a long, long time. If only he could bottle this feeling so that he could keep it for ever. If only he could bottle Raye and keep her with him for ever. That would be true heaven.

'It is beautiful, isn't it?' said Raye.

Liam nodded. 'Yes, it is,' he agreed.

They stood side by side on the cliff top, looking out across the gently rippling sea. They were only about ten metres away from the edge. There were wooden barri-cades further along the cliff edge, where the ground sloped more sharply, but here there was nothing but a warning sign.

'D'you like it here?' asked Liam, moving slowly closer towards the edge.

'At the hotel?'

'Yeah, and the beach and the cliffs and gardens.'

Raye considered. 'Yes, I do actually. But don't tell my parents that, will you?'

'Don't worry, I won't. Do you like it enough to stay . . . for ever?'

'For ever?' Raye said, surprised. 'No one stays anywhere for ever, do they? We all move on at some time – that's just the way life works. What about you? Where's your home?'

'Near here.'

'How come I haven't seen you around before this weekend?'

'I kept to myself,' said Liam. 'And you may not have noticed me, but I certainly noticed you.'

'You did?'

'Of course,' Liam smiled. 'I noticed you from the first day you moved in. You were wearing a red jumper and black jeans and you were arguing with your mum about which room would be your bedroom.'

'You saw all that?' Raye asked, astounded. 'How come you didn't introduce yourself to us? To me? I could've really used a friend when we first moved in.'

'If I could have, I would have. Believe me,' said Liam. 'Were you very lonely?'

Raye nodded and looked away, suddenly self-conscious. 'It took me a long time to settle in.'

'But you got used to it?'

'More than that. I love it here now. It's my home,' smiled Raye. 'Don't you feel the same way about where you live, then?'

'I guess so,' said Liam.

They were now only a metre away from the cliff edge. Liam took another step and stopped. Raye moved to stand beside him.

'Raye, have you ever wanted something so much that you'd do anything to get it? Anything at all?'

'Depends what you mean by anything,' said Raye lightly.

Liam turned to her. 'I suppose it does.' He peered over the edge of the cliff. 'Ever climbed down there?'

'Are you kidding?' Raye scoffed. 'Do I look like a mountain goat?'

'Never been tempted?'

'Nope!'

'Very wise,' Liam smiled. 'But I've got something to show you.'

'What?'

'You have to stand right in front of me or you won't see it properly,' said Liam.

Raye looked at the remaining forty or so centimetres between Liam and the edge of the cliff. 'I'm not sure about that . . .'

'I'll tell you what,' said Liam seriously. 'I promise that if you fall, I'll follow you down.'

'That'll be a great comfort as I break every bone in my body,' Raye said dryly.

'I mean it. I won't let you go alone.'

'So what d'you want to show me?'

'Stand in front of me and then you'll see it.'

Cautiously, Raye moved to stand in front of him, peering gingerly over the cliff top. 'So what am I looking at?'

Liam sidestepped to stand behind and slightly to the side of Raye. 'Look over to the right, about five hundred metres away – just above that ridge,' he said. 'There's a cave just above that ridge . . .'

'That's the one Mr Jackman was trapped in, isn't it?'

Liam nodded. Raye shuddered.

'What about it?'

'I used to use the cave down there as an escape route,' said Liam.

Raye turned to face Liam. 'An escape from what?'

'Life.'

Raye wasn't quite sure what to make of that. 'And did you escape?'

Silence. Raye waited for Liam to answer. The intensity of his expression almost scared her as his eyes burned into hers. But then his expression cleared and his body relaxed as he sighed deeply. 'We'd better be getting back,' he said wearily. 'I'd never forgive myself if anything happened to you.'

'But you didn't answer my question. Did you —?' Before Raye could say another word, someone else interrupted her.

'*Raye, get away from him!*' Nova screamed out from down on the beach.

'What on earth . . .?' Raye turned. 'Nova? What're you doing?'

'Get away from him. He's a ghost. *He's trying to kill you!*' Nova yelled frantically.

'What's she on about?' Raye turned her head to ask Liam.

But Liam's arms were moving towards her, his hands outstretched.

'No!' Raye backed away from him, afraid of what he was about to do. But she stepped off into nothing. Her arms shot out towards Liam, but it was too late. She plummeted downwards.

'RAYE!' Nova screamed.

Raye scrambled desperately for the cliff face. She grabbed hold of an old, thick root, trailing outwards from the cliff face, and gripped it as her hands slid down it. The rough stem scored her skin but she just managed to hold on. Her feet dug against the cliff face, searching for a foothold. She found a tenuous one of sorts in another old root, short and sharp but better than nothing.

Liam fell to the ground and stretched out both hands. 'Raye, reach up and grab hold of my hands.'

'*Raye, don't!*' Nova shrieked out from below her.

Raye screamed as the root she was holding onto cracked and groaned and gave slightly under her weight.

'Raye, whatever you do, don't take his hand!' Nova cried out.

Rainbow looked up at Liam above her. His eyes caught hers and they regarded each other silently. Raye knew in that moment that everything Nova had said was true. She also knew that she was seconds away from falling to her death.

'Rainbow, take my hand. Trust me.' Liam lowered himself even further down until his hand was just centimetres above her own.

'I can't!' Raye screamed. She was terrified of what might happen if she didn't let him help her up, but she was equally terrified of what might happen if she did.

'Take my hand, Rainbow,' Liam ordered, adding with a dry smile, 'I won't let you down!'

'Raye, don't do it!' Nova screamed.

'Please. Trust me,' Liam said softly.

And in that moment it was as if all sound in the world had suddenly stopped. There was just Liam and Rainbow and the silence between them. Raye looked at Liam as he smiled down at her. His silly joke and the words 'trust me' were all she could think of at that moment.

Trust me . . .

Rainbow felt the branch beneath her feet creak and crack and give just a little more. And the root she was holding onto was giving out. She closed her eyes momentarily, then took a deep breath. It was now or never. She reached out and jumped to grab hold of Liam's hand. The root beneath her feet cracked one last time before falling away from the cliff face. Rainbow was left dangling with just Liam's grip between her and a deadly fall.

Immediately Liam tried to haul Rainbow up. He caught hold of her hand with both of his and the strain was evident on his face. But he was doing it. Rainbow pushed herself upwards, her feet braced against the cliff face as Liam struggled to drag her to level ground.

'Liam, don't let her fall!' Nova cried out. 'Please don't let her fall.'

'. . . not . . . going to happen,' Liam grunted, pulling Raye up all the while, until at last he hauled her over the cliff edge and they both lay gasping for breath on the ground.

'I . . . I wasn't going to push you. I was trying to pull you away from the edge,' Liam said when he'd barely got back his breath. 'I wasn't going to do it. I promise.'

Raye looked over at him, still breathing heavily. 'You thought about it, though, didn't you?'

'Only for a second,' Liam admitted.

'Sometimes a second can last a lifetime.'

'And sometimes a lifetime can pass in a second.'

'That's a bit too deep for me right now,' said Raye, still trying to catch her breath. 'But thanks for saving my life, Liam.'

'And thanks for saving mine. Do something for me, Raye. Tell Nova I said . . . eat something!' said Liam.

'Why don't you tell her yourself?' asked Raye, turning her head to face him, only to sit bolt upright and stare.

'I can't.' Liam grinned at her as he slowly faded from view. 'I'm not going to be here for much longer.'

'Wait. Where're you going?' asked Raye urgently.

'No idea! I'm not doing this! Isn't it wonderful?'

Nova ran puffing towards them, having raced all the way up the cliff steps. She stood in front of Raye and Liam as they both got to their feet.

'Liam's leaving us,' Raye said, her voice uneven. 'For good . . .'

Nova turned to Liam, her eyes huge with dismay. 'Aren't you coming back?'

'I don't know, but . . . but I don't think so.'

'But . . . but why're you leaving now? They found your body yesterday. How come you didn't disappear then?' asked Nova.

'Because I was wrong. Leaving this place had nothing

to do with my body being found,' said Liam slowly, still gradually fading from sight. 'It was about what was going on up here –' he tapped his forehead – 'and in here –' he placed a hand over his heart.

'I don't understand,' said Nova.

'Nova —'

'And I don't want to understand – not if it means you'll leave,' Nova admitted in a rush. 'I don't want you to go, Liam.'

'I'll miss you too, Nova,' smiled Liam. 'But it's time for me to move on. At last.'

'But you're the first person to take any notice of me around here.'

'I might've been the first,' said Liam, looking at Raye. 'But I won't be the last. You need to let your family know how you're feeling. Don't bottle things up inside. That was my mistake.'

Liam looked up at the sky, suddenly raising his arms upwards as if he wanted to pull it down and around him. He spun around slowly, his arms still outstretched. When did everything get so *bright*? It was as if he'd spent his entire death with sunglasses on and now they were off and the world was bright and alive and so wonderful. Liam breathed in deeply, feeling he must surely explode with the bliss fizzing inside him. When Raye had fallen over the cliff edge, all he'd wanted to do was reach her and get her to safety. He'd offered up all kinds of silent prayers – like never complaining about being stuck in Phoenix Manor again, just as long as Raye didn't die. How strange that things should work out this way. He turned to Nova, his smile fading slightly when he saw the look on her face. He tried to wipe a tear from her cheek but his finger passed right through it. He bent his head and kissed her. His lips made contact, skin against skin, but when he tried to touch her cheek again, his fingers moved through her as if through mist or a breeze.

'Enjoy your life, Nova. It's very precious,' Liam said softly.

'Raye, do something,' Nova appealed to her sister.

'Don't go . . .' Raye had no idea where the words came from but they spilled out anyway.

Liam's smile was made of pure happiness. 'I have to. I *want* to.'

Raye could hardly see Liam now. He was just a blur through the unexpected tears in her eyes.

'I can't believe I'm outta here at last!' Liam shouted joyfully. 'Raye, you've got a very special sister there. Look after her.'

'I will,' Raye whispered.

'Be happy, Nova,' the last vestige of Liam's image told her. 'And don't be a div-brain all your life. Eat!'

'Wait, Liam. I just want to say . . . goodbye . . .' But she was too late.

He'd gone.

47. Miss Dawn and Miss Eve

Miss Dawn and Miss Eve stood on the front steps of the hotel, watching Nova and Raye walk towards the hotel, arm in arm.

'There you go!' said Miss Dawn smugly. 'He didn't drop her. I knew he'd do the right thing.'

'No, you didn't.'

Miss Dawn laughed. 'All right then, I *hoped* he'd do the right thing. It was always his choice, though.'

'Admit it. He had you worried, didn't he?'

'He certainly did!' Miss Dawn agreed.

'I don't understand him at all,' said Miss Eve. 'If he'd dropped her, he would've had a companion for life – I mean for eternity.'

Miss Dawn shook her head. 'No, he wouldn't. Knowing Raye, she would probably never have spoken to him again. I think she would've hated him for ever. And she wouldn't have been bound to the hotel the way he is. Being stuck at the hotel was his problem to solve, not hers. He would've lost her for good.'

Miss Dawn watched Raye and Nova smile at each other as they carried on walking.

'What about Nova? Is she cured?' asked Miss Eve.

'Of course not. But she's not so alone any more. She's got her family to help her now.'

Miss Eve sighed. 'I'm going to miss Liam. I liked him.'

'Why, Miss Eve, I do believe you're getting soft in your old age,' teased Miss Dawn.

'Never! Come on, old woman. It's time for us to pack up and move on.'

'But we will come back once Mr Clibbens opens the tunnels, won't we?' asked Miss Dawn.

'If we must,' sighed Miss Eve.

'Oh, definitely. They're going to be the biggest tourist attraction for miles around. We can't miss at least one trip through them.'

'What we will miss is our train, if you don't hurry up,' Miss Eve complained.

Miss Dawn watched Nova and Raye for a while longer. 'Good luck to both of you,' she whispered. 'And try not to miss Liam too much.'

'Will you please get a move on?' snapped Miss Eve. 'Nova and Raye won't be that unhappy. They have each other now.'

'I do so love a happy ending!' sighed Miss Dawn.

'I don't!' Miss Eve grumbled. 'So tell me, will they ever see Liam again?'

Miss Dawn turned to Miss Eve and smiled silkily, saying, 'Now that would be telling!'

And the two old women turned round and went back into the hotel.

ABOUT THE AUTHOR

MALORIE BLACKMAN

'Few writers can sustain a plot as well as Malorie Blackman'
Sunday Telegraph

'Blackman is becoming a bit of a national treasure'
The Times

'One of today's outstandingly imaginative and convincing writers'
Junior Bookshelf

Born in London in 1962, Malorie Blackman studied computer science and worked at a variety of different jobs before becoming a full-time writer. Although she has travelled throughout Europe and the United States working as a database manager, her ideal position would be captaining the Starship Enterprise – being a real Star Trek fan – or accompanying agents Mulder and Scully on one of their action-packed X-Files.

Malorie gained phenomenal success with her first book for Transworld, HACKER, which won two major children's awards in 1994: The WHS Mind Boggling Books Award, and the Young Telegraph/Gimme 5 Award. She has written a number of other books for children, including A.N.T.I.D.O.T.E., THIEF!, which has been televised for Book Box for Channel 4 Schools and won the 1996 Young Telegraph/Fully Booked Award, and PIG–HEART BOY, which was shortlisted for the Carnegie Medal and adapted for a Bafta award-winning TV serial. More recently, NOUGHTS & CROSSES won the Children's Book Award, the Sheffield Children's Book Award and the Lancashire Children's Book Award. She has also written a number of books for younger readers.

When she's not working Malorie enjoys messing about on the guitar, piano and saxophone. She goes regularly to the cinema and theatre, enjoys watching TV, playing computer games and surfing the net. She loves reading absolutely everything – except Westerns! She lives in South London with her husband and daughter, Elizabeth.

PIG-HEART BOY
Malorie Blackman

*All I had to do was go downstairs. Or I could call Dad
and tell him that I didn't want to meet Dr Bryce and that
would be the end of that. Life would go on as normal.
And I'd be dead before my fourteenth birthday...*

Cameron is thirteen and desperately in need of a heart
transplant when a pioneering doctor approaches his
family with a startling proposal. He can give Cameron a
new heart — but not from a human donor. From a *pig*.

It's never been done before. It's experimental, risky and
very controversial. But Cameron is fed up with just sitting
on the side of life, always watching and never *doing*. He *has*
to try — to become the world's first pig-heart boy...

'A powerful story about friendship, loyalty and family
around this topical and controversial issue'
Guardian

'Moving but never maudlin,
this is a tale of courage stretched to the limit'
T.E.S.

MADE INTO A BAFTA AWARD-WINNING TV SERIAL

ISBN 0-552-52841- 2

CORGI BOOKS

HACKER
Malorie Blackman

MESSAGE:
THIS IS THE SYSTEM OPERATOR.
WHO IS USING THIS ACCOUNT?
PLEASE IDENTIFY YOURSELF...

When Vicky's father is arrested, accused of stealing over
a million pounds from the bank where he works, she is
determined to prove his innocence. But *how*, when
all the evidence is hidden in computer files?

Helped by her brother Gib and his best friend Chaucy,
Vicky decides to hack into the bank's computers.
For if there is one school subject she is really good at, it is
computing. But even if she does manage to break into the
system, can she find the answers before the real thief finds *her*?

'A fast-moving contemporary adventure'
School Librarian

'Refreshingly new'
Weekend Telegraph

**WINNER OF THE 1994 W H SMITH
MIND-BOGGLING BOOKS AWARD and
THE YOUNG TELEGRAPH/GIMME 5 AWARD FOR
BEST CHILDREN'S BOOK OF THE YEAR**

ISBN 0 552 527513

CORGI BOOKS

A.N.T.I.D.O.T.E.
Malorie Blackman

The words exploded from me in a burst of white-hot anger.
'It's a lie.'

It's a normal Friday evening for Elliot - until the police knock on the door and tell him his mum's in serious trouble! A security video clearly shows her breaking into a giant pharmaceutical company on behalf of A.N.T.I.D.O.T.E., the environmental action group.

Elliot can hardly believe it. His mum's a secretary, isn't she? Not a SPY! And even worse – now she's gone on the run...

'Malorie Blackman has successfully rebooted the ripping yarn'
The Times

'A gripping techno-thriller'
Independent On Sunday

ISBN 0 552 528390

CORGI BOOKS